Two Heads Better Than One?

"Say, you fellas didn't happen to see two other lawdogs out there, somewheres, did you? I was sort of expectin' to meet up with Ransom and Kitchen. In fact, I thought maybe you was them."

"Ransom and Kitchen, huh?" Carson drummed two fingers on his bottom lip, deep lines of feigned thoughtfulness cutting into his forehead. "I don't know . . ." He let his voice trail off as he slid his eyes toward Kilmer.

The curly wolf from Tennessee walked over to Longarm's table, hauled the sack around in front of him, and set it on the table. "Ransom and Kitchen, huh?" he said, parroting Carson. He let the neck of the bag sag toward Longarm, picked up the bottom of the bag, and shook it until two human heads rolled onto the table in front of Longarm. "Could this be them?"

→ TABOR EVANS ←

LONGARM

AND THE HELL CREEK LEAD STORM

JOVE BOOKS, NEW YORK

THE BERKLEY PUBLISHING GROUP
Published by the Penguin Group
Penguin Group (USA) Inc.
375 Hudson Street, New York, New York 10014, USA

Penguin Group (Canada), 90 Eglinton Avenue East, Suite 700, Toronto, Ontario M4P 2Y3, Canada (a division of Pearson Penguin Canada Inc.) • Penguin Books Ltd., 80 Strand, London WC2R 0RL, England • Penguin Group Ireland, 25 St. Stephen's Green, Dublin 2, Ireland (a division of Penguin Books Ltd.) • Penguin Group (Australia), 250 Camberwell Road, Camberwell, Victoria 3124, Australia (a division of Pearson Australia Group Pty. Ltd.) • Penguin Books India Pvt. Ltd., 11 Community Centre, Panchsheel Park, New Delhi—110 017, India • Penguin Group (NZ), 67 Apollo Drive, Rosedale, Auckland 0632, New Zealand (a division of Pearson New Zealand Ltd.) • Penguin Books (South Africa) (Pty.) Ltd., 24 Sturdee Avenue, Rosebank, Johannesburg 2196, South Africa

Penguin Books Ltd., Registered Offices: 80 Strand, London WC2R 0RL, England

This is a work of fiction. Names, characters, places, and incidents either are the product of the author's imagination or are used fictitiously, and any resemblance to actual persons, living or dead, business establishments, events, or locales is entirely coincidental.

LONGARM AND THE HELL CREEK LEAD STORM

A Jove Book / published by arrangement with the author

PRINTING HISTORY
Jove edition / May 2012

ISBN: 978-0-515-15067-4

JOVE®
Jove Books are published by The Berkley Publishing Group, a division of Penguin Group (USA) Inc., 375 Hudson Street, New York, New York 10014. JOVE® is a registered trademark of Penguin Group (USA) Inc. The "J" design is a trademark of Penguin Group (USA) Inc.

PRINTED IN THE UNITED STATES OF AMERICA

10 9 8 7 6 5 4 3 2 1

ALWAYS LEARNING   **PEARSON**

Chapter 1

Longarm's hat blew off his head, but there was no wind.

He scowled. "What in tarna—?"

A rifle cracked in the rocks to his right, echoing around the deep Wyoming canyon he was riding through. The rangy lawman in the brown frock coat and string tie grabbed his Winchester '73 from the scabbard strapped to his McClellan saddle and hurled himself off his left stirrup.

He struck the ground and rolled, his horse whinnying and galloping up the trail, another bullet slamming into the rocks behind him with a wicked screech, the rifle report flatting out hollowly around the canyon. Longarm dove into a niche in the rocks, pumped a round into his Winchester's breech, and edged a look across the trail and at the eroded stone escarpment from where the shot had come.

Dust puffed around a rifle maw. He saw the lap of

red-orange flames. The bullet hammered the rocks to his left, peppering his face with slivers. Longarm raised his Winchester and snapped off five rounds in quick succession—*Bam! Bam! Bam! Bam-Bam!*

A bearded man in checked trousers and a torn brown vest tumbled down the rocks to land at the edge of the trail, bleeding from his face, arms, and chest.

Another rifle cracked behind Longarm. He twisted around, racking a fresh shell into the breech of his Winchester '73, and saw a man in a plaid shirt and battered Stetson running toward him through the rocks and yucca. Longarm fired. His slug slammed into a boulder as the man darted behind it. Longarm gained a knee, pumped a fresh shell, and pressed the stock against his shoulder.

He aimed at the boulder.

His back ached from the impact with the rocky ground. He suppressed the pain and lined up the sites on the boulder's right side and about halfway between the bottom and the top. Presently, the front of a hat brim appeared as the man peeked out from behind the rock. Longarm saw the man's right, deep-set eye and his long nose. The lawman fired. The man's head disappeared for a second before the man stepped out from behind the boulder, his rifle sagging in his arms. The rifle clattered on the rocks. He stumbled out away from the boulder, dragging his boot toes, his bloody head wobbling on his shoulders.

He dropped to his knees and fell forward with a thud.

Longarm ejected the spent cartridge, seated fresh. He waited, looking around at the rocky expanse of high desert stippled with yucca, cedars, and the occasional piñon pine. He'd been tracking three men. Three killers. Where was the third?

A stone dropped past his right shoulder and clattered onto the rocks at his feet.

Longarm threw himself sharply left as a rifle thundered on the top of the butte above him. He rolled off his elbow, saw the long-faced hombre glaring down the smoking barrel of a Spencer repeater at him, and fired twice.

The man grunted, sagged forward, and dropped to the ground in front of Longarm with a loud, cracking thud. He was a big, fat man in a fawn vest and long, black duster. He wore a carefully trimmed gray beard and a patch over his right eye. Blood glistened on the right side of his neck. It pumped from the ragged hole and dribbled thickly over the man's white paper collar.

He thrashed and groaned, stretching his lips back from his teeth. He'd lost his black sombrero, and his bald, freckled pate glistened in the harsh, high-altitude sun. He studied Longarm, his pain-racked eyes brightening with recogniton. "Well, I'll be damned. That you, Longarm?"

"It's me, Dirty Jim."

"Damn you, you murderin' lawdog," he spat through gritted teeth. "You kilt me."

Longarm gained his knees, glared down at the dying brigand, Dirty Jim Reed, and flared his nostrils. "About time someone did."

"Fuck you, Longarm."

"Where's your hostage?"

"Why should I tell you?" Dirty Jim rolled his lone, incredulous, washed-out blue toward Longarm once more. "You come all the way up here from Denver . . . just to hunt us?"

Longarm gained his feet. Holding his rifle in one hand, he brushed dust from his skintight, tobacco tweed trousers with the other, and adjusted the string tie at his throat. "Hell, Dirty, you're right notorious. Don't you know that?"

He picked up his flat-brimmed, snuff-brown hat, poked a finger through the hole in its crown, and scowled.

"I . . . am . . . ?" The prospect of notoriety appealed to the dying brigand. "I thought we was—oh, damn, it hurts!—just small time. Didn't think no famous federal lawdog would hound our trail."

"You crossed a reservation with loot stolen from a mail train and a hostage," Longarm told the man. "That there makes it federal."

"Just my luck," said Dirty Jim. "Got rundown by a famous lawdog and didn't even know the sumbitch was shadowin' me until I'm layin' here like a chicken-thievin' dog, pumpin' my blood out in the hot desert." He sobbed. "Shit!"

"Come on, Dirty Jim," Longarm urged, prodding the man's left shoulder with the square toe of his low-heeled cavalry boot. "Where's your hostage? You don't need her no more. Her family's damn worri—"

Longarm cut himself off. His pleas were landing on deaf ears. Dirty Jim had fallen still, his hands slack against his chest, eyes staring up at the Wyoming sky above Longarm. The sky was a little hazy from a wildfire burning in the lower, fur-carpeted slopes of the Wind River Range to the north.

Longarm scowled. He stepped away from Dirty Jim to inspect the first man he'd shot, Dirty's cousin Melvin Pitts, a rustler and bank robber who'd made a name for himself as a regulator in several past land wars. Seeing that Melvin was as dead as his cousin, Longarm started to walk out to where the third man, H. W. "Chicken" Murphy, lay in a pool of his own blood near a yucca patch trimmed with a rattlesnake skin.

Longarm stopped walking. Frowning, he turned to the south. A rider was galloping over the pale, eroded hills, heading southwest. The girl's long, chestnut hair flew back behind her shoulders, and her long, green skirt buffeted her legs. She glanced toward Longarm from beneath the brim of her man's round-brimmed hat, then batted her heels against her coyote dun's flanks, urging more speed from the horse as she angled away from Longarm.

The lawman lurched forward and swung his rifle over his head, trying to signal the girl she was safe. But it was no use. She climbed a low rise and galloped on down the other side and out of sight.

Longarm cursed and looked vaguely around for the gold coins that the three dead brigands had stolen from a mail puffer in western Utah Territory. Obviously, none of the dead men had the money on him. The group was composed of six men total. The gang had split up when they'd discovered they were being trailed by Longarm and two deputy U.S. marshals out of Montana. The loot might be with the horses of these men or with the other three desperadoes.

Now was not the time to look for it, however.

Glancing south toward where the thieving killers' hostage was fleeing, probably believing that Longarm was another road agent, the lawman jogged up the trail to where his horse, an army remount, was contentedly copping needlegrass. He stepped into the saddle and wasted no time batting his heels against the bay's flanks and galloping across the rolling, sandy, yucca-stippled desert. He thought he knew where the girl was headed. Intending to cut her off, he swung his own mount slightly north, tracing the edge of a shallow canyon that doglegged toward the northwest. Ten minutes later, as the bay was long-striding, chewing up the sage, Longarm saw the girl bound out of the canyon mouth, turning her chestnut head to peer over her right shoulder.

She must have heard Longarm barreling toward her, for she turned to look over her other shoulder. He was close enough to see the horrified expression on her face.

"Hold on!" Longarm shouted, riding crouched low in his McClellan saddle, the brim of his snuff-brown hat bent against his forehead. "I'm law!"

He didn't wonder why the girl couldn't hear him. He couldn't hear himself above the pounding of his own horse's hooves and the wind against his face.

When the girl turned forward, her galloping mount's bridle reins slipped out of her hands to bounce along the ground, bobbing wildly when one of the black's hooves clipped them. She swung an arm down to grab the right ribbon, almost lost her seat, then leaned forward against the black's neck, clutching at the black mane that buffeted her face and looking with terror-creased eyes at Longarm pounding toward her.

He cursed and shook his head, ramming his heels harder against the bay's flanks. The black was a runaway. Even if Longarm could convince the girl he was here to help her, not rape and murder her, she wouldn't be able to stop the black. The horse had its head. It had no more use for the horse and rider thundering toward it than the girl did.

Fortunately, the black didn't have the bottom of Longarm's bay. He closed on it quickly, angling toward it from the right. The girl looked back at him once more.

"No!" she cried. The slit in her riding skirt opened to reveal a long stretch of smooth, creamy thigh.

Only vaguely appreciating the image, Longarm put the bay up beside the black. When his left thigh was even with the black's neck, he reached forward and down to his left, and grabbed the bridle reins.

"Go away, damn you!" the girl screamed.

Longarm quickly wrapped his reins around his saddlehorn then slipped his right boot free of its stirrup. He placed his right knee atop his saddle then used that knee to slide himself off his own horse's bouncing back and onto the back of the black, just behind the girl. The bay slanted away from the black, and Longarm leaned forward against the girl's slender back, sort of cradling her in his arms while sawing back on the reins.

"Whooooahhhhhhh, horse! Whoa, now! Whooooo-ahhhhhhhh!"

The girl's body felt warm and supple until, as the horse slowed, she started hammering at Longarm with her elbows.

"Leave me!" she screamed. "Leave me alone, damn you!"

Longarm put his head down against the girl's rich, curly, chestnut hair and endured her flailing arms until he got the black stopped. "Hold on there! Hold on there, miss!"

"I'll kill you! I'll kill you!"

"You don't understand!" Longarm got his arms wrapped around her writhing body from behind, pressing her own arms against her sides. "I'm tryin' to tell you—"

Just then she jerked back, wrenching her right arm free and smashing that elbow against Longarm's right cheek.

"Ow!"

Stunned, the lawman loosened his grip. The girl pivoted right, and then suddenly, limbs entangled, they tumbled down the side of the horse together. The ground came up to smack Longarm hard about the head and shoulders. The girl had somehow gotten twisted around, and she landed on top of him facing his boots.

Her skirt had come up over his head, like a collapsed tent, and his face was pressed against the inside of her bare right thigh. The leg was warm, smooth as soap. As the girl groaned, pressing the two soft lumps of her breasts against his crotch, he glimpsed a few tufts of hair from her silky, dark brown snatch poking out from beneath her cream silk bloomers that had gotten pulled up taut against her alluring pink crack. Reluctantly, Longarm reached up to slide the girl's legs off his head, and her skirt came away from her face. She'd been momentarily stunned by the fall, but now she was struggling again, trying to crawl away on her elbows and knees, sobbing in terror.

"Leave me alone! You leave me alone! Oh, God, out of the frying pan and into the fire!"

Chapter 2

"Hold on, miss!" Longarm thought he remembered hearing that the girl's name was Bella something-or-other, who'd been traveling with her father when Dirty Jim's bunch attacked the train and took her hostage to hold a posse at bay. "I'm a deputy United States marshal, galldangit."

She squirmed around and was beating him about the head and shoulders with her tightly clenched fists, bunching her lips and narrowing her eyes. Longarm held up his arms to shield himself from the blows. Suddenly, she stopped, frowning at him skeptically. He looked at her, saw that her eyes were lilac blue and enticingly long and slanted. The left one was charmingly a little off-center.

"You're . . . who . . . ?"

"Deputy United States Marshal Custis P. Long out of Denver's First District Court." Longarm lowered his arms and licked a small blood drip from his lower lip. The girl stared at him, narrowing one eye and turning her head to one side skeptically. "How do I know?"

"Here."

He fished his wallet out of his coat pocket and flipped it open to reveal the silver-chased moon-and-star badge pinned inside. The girl gasped, jerking head back sharply and splaying one pale, long-fingered, well-manicured hand across her ample bosom that was partly revealed, Longarm couldn't help noticing, by several missing buttons and a tear in her pink muslin blouse. She lifted her eyes from the badge and studied him carefully, eyes darting this way and that across his face. Suddenly, with a relieved sob, she threw herself against him, burying her head in his broad chest and wrapping her arms around him, holding him so tightly that for a moment he had trouble drawing a full breath.

"It's all right, Miss, uh . . . Bella, is it?" Longarm had always been an awkward hugger, though he couldn't help enjoying the push of the girl's two firm mounds against his chest. He patted her back like a friendly uncle and ignored the pull in his groin. "Everything's gonna be just fine. Have you back home in no time."

"Oh, God, it was awful!" she said, keeping her cheek pressed taut against him and squirming against him enough to make the annoying tug in his groin pull harder. "I thought I was a goner! I really thought I was a goner." Her shoulders jerked as she sobbed.

"Well, it's all over now. Safe as a lamb in a manger, Miss Bella."

"Just awful!"

"There, there!"

"They . . ." She let her voice trail off, punctuated by a quiver and a sob.

"I'm sure they did," Longarm allowed, knowing that as depraved a bunch as Dirty Jim's could not have resisted the girl's charms, not to mention her supple, comely body. He could still feel the press of her bare, warm thigh against his mustached-mantled mouth, causing a frightening warmth to join the hard pull in his groin. He wrapped his hands around her arms and gently pushed her away. "I'm sure they did terrible things, but you can forget about it now. You're safe with me, Miss Bella."

"Oh, the horror!" She sniffed and swiped the back of her hand across her nose, giving those lilac blues to Longarm, frowning shamefully. "It was just awful what they did to me, Marshal. I'm so ashamed. And then . . ." Her gaze acquired an accusing cast and she pressed her elbows to her heaving bosom. "Oh, God—was that your mustache I felt against my bare leg?"

She reached down and pressed her dusty skirt firmly against the appendage in question.

"Was that your leg? I do apologize. It all happened so fast, I didn't notice. Here, let me help you, Miss Bella. You ain't hurt, are you? That was quite a tumble we took."

"No, I don't think so." The girl stood and, holding her blouse closed with one hand, adjusted her skirt with the other, brushing away the dust and sand. "After all I've been through, Marshal Long, I reckon I oughta be grateful I'm not dead."

"Please call me Longarm, Miss Bella. Most folks do."

"Longarm." She brushed her chestnut locks from her lilac eyes and quirked her long, red lips with a bemused little smile, letting her left eye wander charmingly toward her nose. "What a strange name. Well, I do apologize for running away from you, Longarm, but I thought you were just another cutthroat out to kill those three brigands and steal their guns and horses as well as myself, as you can well imagine."

"I understand." Longarm stooped to pluck his hat off the ground. He swatted it against his thigh, puffing dust. "What about the loot they stole from the train, Miss Bella? Was Dirty Jim carrying it? I figure maybe he left it with his horses before him and them other two bushwhacked me."

"Oh, I wouldn't know about any loot, Longarm. Those three had me so frightened I couldn't think about much of anything except how broken-hearted my father and mother and little Susie would be when they learned that those depraved coyotes finally got tired of me and threw me in the nearest ravine for the bobcats to chew!"

"That's not gonna happen now, miss." Longarm inspected the horse's hocks and cannons to make sure it hadn't gone lame in the girl's wild ride across the desert, or that its frogs hadn't picked up any cactus thorns or stones. "We'll ride on back to where I left Dirty Jim. Likely have to spend the night there, I'm afraid. The sun'll be down in an hour. We'll get started on the trail back to Fort Keogh tomorrow, get you on a train and have you back in the loving arms of Ma and Pa and little Sue in a few days."

She gave another relieved gasp and threw herself into Longarm's broad chest once more. "I don't know how to thank you, Marshal!"

Longarm glanced across the southern desert toward distant mountains rising darkly along the border of Colorado, squinting his keen brown eyes as he tried to pick up any dust plumes that might indicate his two cohorts, Marshals J. T. Ransom and Homer Kitchen. Ransom and Kitchen had headed south on the tails of the other three of Dirty Jim's bunch, with the intention of meeting up with Longarm again at Hog's Head Stage Station after the three lawmen had run down their quarry.

"Nonsense. Let's get you back on your horse." Longarm placed his hands around the girl's slender waist and lifted her into the saddle. "Up you go."

"Oh, gosh," she said with a thrilled chuckle. "You did that so easily, as though I weighed no more than a tumbleweed." She smiled at Longarm, her pretty lilac eyes flashing in the late, golden light. "I was certainly lucky to have had such a big, capable lawman ride to my rescue, Longarm!"

"Aw, hell," Longarm said, feeling a faint warmth in his cheeks as he walked out to where his bay stood in the shade of a lone cottonwood.

He and the girl rode back to where Melvin Pitts lay sprawled across the trail and Dirty Jim and Chicken Murphy moldered nearby.

A coyote was sniffing around Dirty Jim's ears. Another one of the gray brush wolves slinked toward the dead outlaws through the rocks north of the trail.

The one investigating Dirty Jim put his head down and showed his teeth at Longarm and the girl, and then gave a frustrated whimper before turning and trotting off toward a near ravine. The other turned then, as well, and both were gone, though not for long, Longarm knew. The carrion-eaters would likely be back just as soon as Longarm pulled out.

He had no intention of taking the time to bury the trio. One, it would be dark soon and he needed to find a camp for himself and the girl. Two, he didn't feel like working that hard in the hot sun. Three, after what they'd done to poor Miss Bella, they didn't deserve any semblance of a proper burial.

While the girl frowned in revulsion from the black's saddle, Longarm checked over each body to see if any of them were carrying any of the stolen train loot. None was. Their weapons would have been of use, of course, but he didn't want the bay to have to carry the additional weight. Besides, Longarm's own double-action, Frontier Model Colt .44, positioned for the cross draw on his left hip, and his Winchester '73, as well as the double-barreled derringer he kept hidden inside his right vest pocket, connected by a gold-washed chain to the fob in the opposite pocket, were all the weaponry he required. The way he saw it, men who burdened themselves with more smoke wagons than they could shoot at one time were underskilled or showing off.

He left the dead men and their weapons where they'd fallen, then had the girl lead him to where Dirty Jim and his ilk had tied their horses in a shallow, brush-lined wash about fifty yards south of the trail. When he'd unsaddled the three mounts and left them to forage and seek water on their own—likely some local shotgun rancher would adopt the critters—he stepped into his saddle once more and led the girl off in search of a camp.

A half hour later he and Miss Bella rode down into a lime-green valley with a meandering stream lined by rabbitbrush, firs, ponderosa pines, and cottonwoods as well as the occasional ash and box elder. He'd figured the girl could do with a bath, and he wouldn't mind washing some of the trail dust from his own six-foot-three-inch frame of knotted gristle and hard muscle. He was sunburned and sweat-soaked, and he smelled like he belonged in a hider camp.

Also, he could do with some fresh, cool branch water to mix with a couple shots of Maryland rye, a bottle of which was riding in his saddlebags.

"Will this do?" Longarm asked the girl as they walked their horses toward a horseshoe bend well concealed by trees and shrubs. The stream lay beyond the foliage—a strip of blue velvet trimmed with white lace. The water murmured beneath the fresh sound of the cooling breeze in the branches.

"Quite nicely. Thank you again, Longarm."

"Ah, don't mention it, Miss Bella." He moved the bay through the trees then swung down from his saddle. "I'll tend the horses if you want to freshen up. I saw a well-concealed hole just around the next bend yonder. Don't worry—if you run into trouble, give a shout and I'll come shootin'."

The girl smiled and stepped down from her own saddle. "That's a wonderful idea."

"By the time you get back, I'll have a fire going. Oh, and I have a cake of soap and a towel in my saddlebags. Help yourself."

"You're spoilin' me, now!"

She smiled winningly, rummaged around in his saddlebags, then turned away with soap and towel and ran skipping through the trees. Longarm stared after her, one brow arched pensively. Then he finished tending the horses and headed off to gather wood. He spied a big jackrabbit foraging in a growing patch of shade, and shot it—a clean pistol shot through the animal's head, killing it instantly and painlessly.

"Longarm, was that you?" the girl called from the stream.

"Me shootin' supper, Miss Bella. All's well!"

"Oh, God, I'm so hungry!"

Longarm carried the wood and the rabbit back to the campsite, a well-sheltered place among the pines where he'd spread his gear over the soft bed of forest duff. The stream murmured through the brush about ten yards away. Squirrels chattered in the branches, and crows cawed on the other side of the canyon, their cries echoing off the far, sandstone ridge.

Longarm built a small fire. He cleaned the rabbit and skewered it on a spit he'd fashioned from green willow limbs then sat back against a log with a weary yawn. He poured himself a few fingers of Maryland rye in a tin cup, added cool, fresh water from the stream, and plucked a three-for-a-nickel cheroot from the breast pocket of his frock coat. He bit off the end, plucked a burning twig from the fire, and lit the cigar. Through the puffing smoke he spied the girl moving toward him, meandering through the trees.

Longarm dipped his chin and studied her skeptically from beneath his thick, brown brows, trying to suppress the old, familiar pull in his loins.

The former hostage of Dirty Jim's randy bunch wore nothing except for Longarm's towel, which covered her only from mid-chest to mid-thigh. She held her clothes in one pale arm and pinched the towel closed between her breasts with her other hand. They made the towel bulge invitingly. Her hair had been wet, but now it was drying and sliding around in the breeze, bouncing across her naked shoulders.

"Miss Bella," Longarm said, sucking the rich cigar smoke deep into his lungs, "you ain't wearin' all that much."

Chapter 3

The girl smiled, her pale cheeks blushing and dimpling beautifully, the late, golden light dancing in her lilac eyes. "I do apologize, Longarm."

She stopped a few feet from the fire and dropped her eyes demurely. Her thighs were still damp, and they glistened wetly in the firelight. "I couldn't resist the urge to wash my clothes in that lovely stream. Would you mind terribly if I sat around the fire in nothing more than my towel . . . just until my clothes have dried in front of the fire, of course? Please, sir, I know—you're being a lawman an' all—that I can trust you to be a gentleman. And please don't think me a harlot!"

"I reckon you've been through a lot, Miss Bella. Far be it for me to deny you the comfort of clean duds. I reckon if you can put your faith in my ability to restrain myself from removing said towel and doing such things as wouldn't be decent"—he puffed the cigar, stared at her bemusedly through the wafting smoke—"I reckon I'd be no better than Dirty Jim and his ilk if I did otherwise, wouldn't I?"

Her smile faded a little as she stared back at him obliquely. Then she smiled her coquettish smile once more. "I knew I could trust you, Longarm."

Strutting about the camp in only the towel, she began spreading her clothes over rocks and hanging them from branches. She had a devil of a time keeping the towel in place as she did so. In fact, it slid down her chest a couple of times, but she managed to catch it before her breasts were totally exposed.

"You need any help, there, Miss Bella?"

As she hung her skirt from a pine branch, she glanced over her shoulder at him. The towel slipped down once more past her right breast, so that the lawman could see the entire side of the firm, pale orb and part of the tender pink aureole.

"Whoops!" the girl said, blushing and giggling. "No, I can manage!"

When she finished, she came over to the fire and dropped to her knees, widening her lilac eyes at the sputtering, crackling rabbit. "That smells heavenly!" she intoned.

"And about done," Longarm said.

Fighting the boner in his pants, he plucked the rabbit off the fire, split the carcass in two equal halves down the middle lengthwise, and set each on a tin plate charred and dented from many campfires.

Damn this girl, he thought, wincing at the hard pull in his shorts. She wasn't making it easy for him to main-

tain his professional dignity. He'd known some co-
quettes in his time, but this one took the cake. He could
tell by the quick, furtive glances she slid toward him,
wistfully sucking her bottom lip, that she was enjoying
his misery.

He gave her one of the plates of steaming rabbit, and
she dug in hungrily. Longarm sat down on the other side
of the fire from her, lifted the rabbit off his plate, and
began chewing the meat off the bones. The girl ate like
a famished gandy dancer, with such abandon that her
towel slipped down her chest several more times, once
fully exposing her breasts before she noticed, feigned
embarrassment and chagrin, and pulled it back up, before wiping her greasy hands on her bare thighs.

"Sure is good, Longarm," she said as she ate noisily.
"Don't think I've ever been so hungry in my whole life."
She looked across the fire at him. "Don't quite know
how to thank you for all you've done for me."

"Just doin' my job, Miss Bella."

"Now you're just being modest."

When she finished the meal, she licked her fingers,
stood with a grunt, holding the towel in place, and came
across the fire. "Allow me to do my share."

She let her fingers brush across his thigh as she
closed her hand on his plate.

"You're so scantily clad, Miss Bella, mayhaps I'd
best—"

"Oh, shush. I'm just gonna take these over to the river
and give 'em a quick washing. I'll be back in a minute."

Longarm sat back against the log with a ragged sigh
as he watched the girl walk away through the brush, her

legs long and fine, her feet delicate and pink. Her thick, chestnut hair flowed down her slender back in rich, delectable waves.

When she came back, she was carrying the plates, but she wasn't wearing the towel. She carried it down low by her side, letting it trail along the ground behind her. Her breasts were deep and full, the nipples with large aureoles slanting slightly away from each other. Her belly was pleasantly plump, her hips round and matronly. She might have been a girl of twenty or so, but her body was all woman. The womanly need fairly radiated off her pale skin that, now that night had fallen, the fire caressed lovingly.

She stopped at the edge of the fire, regarding him gravely, one brow arched, and dropped the towel on the ground near Longarm's neatly stacked firewood.

Longarm took a sip from his Maryland rye and branch water, and wiped a hand across his thick longhorn mustache. "Miss Bella, you done dropped your towel."

She stuck the tip of her finger between her teeth and bit down on it. "Oops."

Then she came toward him and knelt down beside him. "You're thinking I am a harlot, after all."

"You're the one who's naked, Miss Bella."

"You said it yourself. I've been through a lot. I want to thank you for your help in the best way I can." Bella dropped her hand to his belly and tucked her fingers behind his cartridge belt. "Lest you think I'm just being selfless, I want you to know that I'm right attracted to you, Longarm. You're a big, handsome, honorable man.

I want you to make love to me and help me forget how savagely I've been treated over the past several days."

"Now, Miss Bella," Longarm said, shifting his weight on his buttocks to relieve some of the pressure of his tight pants on his crotch, "you know that wouldn't be professional."

She smiled as she unbuckled his cartridge belt and then slipped the gun and belt out from around his waist. "I'll never tell. And it'd mean so much to me . . . to allow you to comfort me this night, Longarm."

She laid her open hand on his crotch. He could feel the warmth of it through his trousers. It bit him deep. He heard himself groan as she massaged his iron shaft pushing against the tight fabric. "You're so . . . big."

The ground rose and fell around Longarm as she caressed him, leaning close so that her breasts slanted out from her chest to brush his shoulder. He could see a slight mole, little more than a blemish, on the side of the right one. That nipple glowed in the flickering firelight. Her hair shone like honey. She parted her lips slightly as she watched her hand caressing his hardness through his pants, her hair sliding back and forth along the sides of her face.

Longarm could smell the earthy ripeness of her.

He raised his hand and slid her hair back from her face, caressed her smooth cheek with his thumb. She glanced at him, smiled, then used both hands to open the buttons of his fly. She spread it open with one while she reached in with the other and closed her fist around him. His cock had pushed out from the fly of his summer-weight long underwear bottoms, and his bare flesh thrilled at her warm squeeze. As she pulled it out of his pants, his heart throbbed with each slow pump of her small, pale hand.

After she'd worked him into a fever, perspiration beading his brow, she tossed her head back, glanced at him coyly, then lowered her head toward his belly. She held his cock in her right hand as she slid her mouth ever-so-excruciatingly-slowly over the bulging mushroom head. Her tongue was wet and hot, her lips silky smooth, as she slid her mouth down the length of him, until the head of the shaft had pushed as far as it could go down her throat and she made a little gagging sound.

She pulled her head back and looked up at him, eyes crossing, lips wet, breasts rising and falling as she breathed. "So big," she rasped, before closing her mouth over him once more.

Longarm groaned, rested his elbows back atop the log behind him, and groaned once more.

Her head bobbed faster, faster. Her tongue slithered across him, probing, prodding, teasing. She giggled, cooed, grunted, gagged. When he was approaching climax, he pulled her up by her shoulders, stood, looked around carefully to make sure they were alone out there, then quickly shucked off his clothes. He lay her down on his bedroll, spread her legs with his own, and fucked her good and proper, until she lay quivering and spent beneath him, sliding her heels from his back and slowly lowering her legs to the ground.

"Oh, God," she said as he rolled off of her, breathing hard. "Oh, Jesus, Longarm."

"My sentiments exactly, Miss Bella."

She hooked a leg over his, shook her hair back, and rested her head on his chest, twirling a finger in the cinnamon hair curling across the heavy slabs of his broad chest. The night was cool, but her body was warm and slick with perspiration. Her breath was hot against his skin.

"Can we do it again before we go to sleep?"

Longarm was tired, and it was late. But he wasn't that tired, and it wasn't that late. He chuckled as he closed his hands over the taut globes of her buttocks. "Why not?"

After a few minutes of kissing and fondling, they did it again, her straddling him, him kneading her jostling breasts.

Then they rolled apart and slept, curled on their sides.

Longarm had no idea how much time had passed when he felt her stir beside him. He kept his eyes closed until he heard the familiar ratcheting click of a cocking gun hammer. He opened his eyes. She stood over him, naked, extending his own Colt at him with both hands. She narrowed her eyes and bunched her lips. "This is for Dirty Jim, Melvin, and Chicken, you law-bringin' son of a bitch!"

Click! Click! Click! Click-click-click!

Six times, the hammer pinged on an empty chamber.

Bella stared in hang-jawed exasperation at the empty gun in her hand.

Longarm grinned up at her, blinked slowly. "Took the bullets out while you was bathin', Miss Bella. I wasn't sure, you understand, but a girl as horny as you after what you been through usually harbors a secret or two."

He scissored a leg out, cutting her own feet out from under her. She hit the ground on her ass with an indignant scream. The wind of her fall caused the near-dead coals to glow and spark. Dust and pine needles blew up around her.

"Bastard!"

"You were in on the holdup the whole time," Longarm said, gaining his feet and walking naked over to his saddlebags, out of which he pulled his handcuffs and a rope coil. "This ain't my first time on the ole merry-go-round, ya understand."

She was sobbing angrily as he turned her over on her belly and breasts, wrenched her arms behind her back, and cuffed her. Then he dragged her across the camp and used the rope to tie her ankles to a pine tree.

Slipping into his balbriggans, he regarded her crying with her forehead pressed against her knees. "Now, if you don't mind," he said, "I'd like to catch a few winks before hauling your crooked ass back to Utah Territory for trial."

She mashed her feet against the ground and cried, cursing him.

Longarm gave her his back as he curled onto his side, rested his head against his saddle, and slept.

Chapter 4

Late the next night, a witch's finger of blue-white lightning forked out of the black, rainy sky and pounded the ridge on the north side of the canyon with a wicked, echoing crack and catlike snarl. There was an explosion like a detonated keg of dynamite that quickly died, leaving tongues of blue electricity licking along the top of the ridge and several feet down the side of it. Amid the light, Longarm saw several silhouetted rocks tumble down the ridge, clattering and thundering toward the canyon floor.

Longarm's bay stopped along the stage road that he and the depraved Miss Bella Flowers were following toward the Hog's Head Stage Station on Hog's Head Creek. The horse whinnied and pranced as the rocks plunged to the canyon floor a hundred yards to the right. Too far away to do either him or his rider any harm, but

the horse didn't know that. Horses hated storms nearly
as much as they hated wildcats.

Longarm wasn't partial to either, himself.

Neither did the girl care for the storm, judging by her
scream when the lightning had struck. Now she shouted,
"Damn you, Lawdog—I'm cold and wet and I want to
find shelter this fucking instant!"

The lawman glanced over his shoulder at her riding
tied to the black behind him. In the silver light of the
storm, with its rain slashing the darkness like streaks
of quicksilver, she looked like a drowned rat. Her hat
had blown down her back, where it hung by a horsehair
thong from her neck. Her cuffed hands were tied to her
saddle horn, so she couldn't put it on again. Little good
it would do her, anyway. She was already soaked to the
gills, her hair plastered to her head and shoulders.

"Keep your shorts on, Miss Bella," Longarm yelled
above the pounding rain. "The Hog's Head Station is up
here . . . somewhere," he added, turning his head forward
to stare along the muddy trail that had become a virtual
arroyo, water swirling up around his horse's fetlocks.

He touched his heels to the bay's flanks and pulled
the black along by its bridle reins, continuing up the
road. The two-track trace wound around a long bend in
the black canyon wall, and when the wall pulled back
on the right, the lawman was relieved to see a splash of
dull amber light ahead. He and the girl continued toward
the light. Longarm watched it grow and slide to the left
side of the trail, until he could make out the low-slung
cabin sitting there at a broad spot in the canyon floor,
fronted by a narrow porch, off the near end of which a

rain barrel sat, catching the moisture from a makeshift trough angling down from the roof.

An olla hung down from the porch roof. The clay water vessel swung this way and that in the wind, and two rocking chairs rocked wildly, as though agitated ghosts were in them.

To the left was a broad barn with a loft and a hitch-and-rail corral abutting it. There were no horses in the corral. Likely the fresh stage team was inside the barn. A wheelless Concord coach sat in front of the corral near a stock trough, the frequent lightning flashes and the dull light from the station house's front windows winking off its sides. A windmill stood in the middle of the yard, wooden blades spinning and clattering, nickel-sized raindrops splashing in the overfilled tank before it.

Longarm reined the bay over to the barn, then swung down from the saddle into the soft mud that washed up over his boots, and pulled open one of the big, wooden doors. He led the bay and the black inside, then scratched a dry match to life on his thumbnail and lit an old bull's-eye lantern hanging from a ceiling support post.

The light pushed shadows back into the barn's musty depths, flashing on horses' ghostlike eyes, directed at him suspiciously from stalls lining the alley, and on feed bins and water troughs. He replaced the lantern's chimney and pulled the barn door closed behind him, dulling the storm's roar, though still hearing the rain pounding the loft roof. There was the tinny plopping of water leaking through the roof and loft floor and onto the hard-packed earth near Longarm's muddy boots.

He looked around the barn, wondering if any of the dozen or so horses he saw belonged to the two lawmen he was hoping to meet up with. Them and, hopefully, the other three members of Dirty Jim's gang and the loot they'd stolen from the mail train.

"Hey, asshole!" the girl shouted indignantly, hunched inside her oversized, brown wool coat, lilac eyes glistening in the lantern light. "You gonna cut me down from here or leave me here to catch my death of cold?"

"It ain't much warmer down here," Longarm said, plucking his folding Barlow knife from his pants pocket, flicking out the blade, and reaching up to cut the girl's hands free of her saddle horn.

"I need a warm fire and some hot coffee. And I need to get out of these wet clothes, you mangy sonofabitch!" Holding her cuffed hands in front of her, she leaned toward him, jutting her chin at him like an enraged wolverine. "But don't get any ideas. I don't care if you're hung like a goddamn army mule—I've fucked you for the last time!"

"Oh, my! Oh, my!" a man's voice grumbled thickly from deep in the barn's shadows. "Who's there? Oh, my goodness. Such talk." The man's silhouette took shape in the barn's alley—a bent, lurching figure, boots scuffing on the straw-flecked floor. "Is that a girl using such language?"

"A girl but not a lady, Jeff," Longarm told the oldster stepping into the edge of the lantern light. "This here is Miss Bella Flowers. I won't mince words—she's bad. Part of the Dirty Jim Reed gang that robbed a mail puffer out Utah-way. Her poor father, whom she was riding the train with, didn't know about her evil doin's, but he will now." Longarm pulled the girl brusquely down from her saddle and set her on the barn floor. "And I also suspect it won't come as a big surprise his dear little Bella wasn't all sugar and spice."

"Fuck you."

"Dear Lord," said the sixty-year-old hostler, who made his home in a rear lean-to addition to the Hog's Head Station horse barn, and whom Longarm had come to know over the many years he'd passed through this Wyoming country. Clad in a battered hat, wash-worn balbriggans, and ancient mule-eared boots, he had several striped blankets thrown over his bowed shoulders. "I never heard a girl talk that way. Even a bad one, and I've known my fill of girls I wouldn't call good, per se."

"Fuck you, too, old man."

Jeff Thigpen fingered his scraggly gray goat beard and stared at the girl as though she'd dropped down out of the sky and was speaking an alien tongue.

"Well, here's another one," Longarm told him. "You got some duds she can wear till these dry, Jeff? This hydrophobic polecat'll be spending the night out here with me, I'm afraid. I'll be out later. Don't worry—I'll have her trussed up like a calf for the branding."

The girl cut loose with another long string of obscenities so loudly that she drowned out the storm. When she was done, the old man twitched his washed-out brown eyes at Longarm, and said, "Damn, if she hasn't taken me to school!"

Longarm chuckled as he set his wet McClellan atop a stall partition. "Gotta admit, she taught me a few new cuss words my ownself. Say, you ain't seen them other two badge-toters I rode in with the other night, have you, Jeff? We're all supposed to powwow here before heading back Utah-way."

"Neither hide nor hair, Longarm," the oldster said, glancing once more skeptically at Bella Flowers as he turned and ambled back toward his lean-to.

When Longarm had tended to Bella, leaving her dryly clothed and tied to a support post in the barn, he headed back out into the driving rain, meandering around the largest puddles in the yard as he made his way to the station house. Atop the porch he scraped as much mud from his boots as he could on a braided hemp rug, then pushed through the storm door and inside, where a couple of flickering lamps shunted shadows and revealed that the place was empty.

Empty except for the stationmaster, Ralph Ledger, who sat at a table near a ticking woodstove in the middle of the long room. A pot gurgled and chugged atop the cookstove, hot brown juice bubbling out from beneath the lid and sending the aroma of cooked beans and venison into the room. The scarred bar and the back bar with its warped, cracked mirror lay against the right wall. The floor was covered with mud-flecked sawdust, showing the prints of previous patrons.

"Well, look what the cat dragged in," the stationmaster said, looking up from the plate of meat and beans he was hunkered over.

He was a big, hard-bellied man with thick, curly,

salt-and-pepper hair that hung down across the collar of his soiled work shirt. Muttonchop whiskers of the same color framed his tan, fleshy face. A dark brown mustache mantled his broad, thick-lipped mouth. He continued to eat hungrily, shoveling in the beans and meat as though he were enjoying his last meal, and jerked a thumb of his free hand at the once fancy, now dusty and scratched European clock ticking hollowly behind the bar. The hands were nearly straight up, showing a few minutes past midnight.

"You keep long hours, Custis."

"And I got little enough to show for it." Longarm held his hat straight out, letting the water run off the brim and onto the scarred, dusty floor. "You ain't seen Ransom and Kitchen, have ya?"

"Nope. They're headed back this way, are they?"

"The gang split up, so we did, too. Arranged to meet back here once we run them cutthroats to ground."

"You run your bunch to ground?"

"Indeed I did. One's still breathin'."

"Imagine that!"

Longarm removed his rain slicker and hung it over a chair near the ticking woodstove. "Give me a plate of that, will ya?"

Ledger dropped his fork with a tinny *ping!* on his empty plate and rose heavily from his chair. "Anything for law and order."

As he walked around behind the bar, Longarm walked to a table near the stove, kicked out a chair that faced the front door and windows, and sagged heavily

into it. Ledger brought a plate over to the stove, filled it
with the steaming stew, and set it, with a shot glass and
a beer, on the table in front of the lawman.

"That there's on the house, Custis. Just a little show
of appreciation for the job you do, at least tryin' to rid
this canker on the devil's ass, known as the Great Amer-
ican Frontier, of killers, thieves, and general miscre-
ants!"

"I'll be damned if you ain't gone all poetic on me,
Ralph!"

Ledger chuckled and kicked a chair out across from
Longarm then stopped and turned his head toward the
front door. Longarm had taken his first bite of the hot,
succulent stew, but now he stopped chewing as he stared
toward the front of the place, as well. He, too, had heard
the splashing thuds of approaching riders.

Continuing to chew his food, he said, "That'd be
them now, most likely. Better fill another couple of
plates, Ralph, and break out the bourbon. Them two are
bourbon drinkers."

Longarm heard the riders milling for a minute or two
outside the front of the station house. They were speaking beneath the hammering of the rain on the roof, so
Longarm couldn't make out what they were saying. He
was a little puzzled that the two lawmen—if that's who
they were—didn't take their horses to the barn. Maybe
they wanted to see if Longarm was here before they
tended their stock.

Presently, boots thudded on the porch boards. The
front door came open and a man stepped in—a tall, lean
man with a dragoon-style mustache and close-set eyes

beneath the dripping brim of his soiled cream Stetson. Longarm saw right off that he was neither J. T. Ransom nor Homer Kitchen.

Neither was the second or third man who came in behind the first, the third man closing the door on the storm, while the lightning flashed behind him, reflecting off the bluing of the sawed-off, double-barreled, ten-gauge shotgun hanging down his back by a leather lanyard. Longarm took another bite of the stew with his left hand, casually reaching under the table with his other hand to release the keeper thong over his Colt's hammer.

Nope, none of these three was one of the lawmen he'd hoped to meet here.

They were, indeed, the three cutthroats that Ransom and Kitchen had gone after.

Chapter 5

The first of the three cutthroats to enter the saloon Longarm recognized as Ben Carson. The second was Klute Kilmer—about Carson's height but thicker and with a slight paunch under his india rubber raincoat. He was dressed all in black except for a red bandanna. The last man was the Mexican, Ernesto Santiago. He was the one with the sawed-off, double-barrel greener.

The three stood in a line in front of the door, facing Longarm, their hats and coats dripping on the floor.

The stationmaster, Ralph Ledger, had turned away from Longarm's table to study the newcomers. Now, shuttling his fearful gaze between the three outlaws and Longarm, he walked slowly sideways toward the bar and out of the line of fire, kicking a chair as he went.

Longarm studied the three cutthroats—Carson on Longarm's left nearest the bar, Kilmer in the middle, Santiago on the right. Kilmer held the neck of a burlap bag thrown over his left shoulder. His rain slicker was tucked back behind the walnut grips of a Colt Army revolver jutting from the holster thonged on his right thigh, which was clad in wet, black denim. Two inches of the blue-steel barrel protruded from the bottom of the holster.

"Wet one tonight," Longarm said, taking one more slow, casual forkful of the stew and then setting the fork down on his empty plate.

"Ain't it?" said Carson.

He was the leader of the other two. He'd been second-in-command of the gang beneath Dirty Jim, both hailing from the hills of Tennessee. He looked at Ledger and said, "Set us up. Whiskey."

"I recommend the stew," Longarm said, keeping both his hands on the table, extending his arms out on either side of his plate. He maintained a casual expression, but his keen brown eyes watched the three killers closely, ready for any sign that one was about to, or two or all three were about to, jerk iron. "Ralph makes the best stew in Wyoming. I've been eating it for years."

"Might just have us some," said Kilmer, his gray-yellow eyes staring straight across the room at Longarm. He had enormous ears but a small nose and weak chin, giving him a crazy, inbred look. His broad cheeks wore two or three days of wiry, dark brown beard stubble. "Later," he added, opening and closing his hand around the neck of the croaker sack dangling down his back.

"First we'll have a drink." Carson looked at Ledger, who stood leaning back on his elbows propped atop the bar, regarding the cutthroats skeptically. "Mr. Ledger, you need your ears cleaned out for you?"

The stationmaster swept Longarm with his faintly inquiring gaze then turned and walked around behind the bar. As he set out three shotglasses, Carson glanced across Kilmer at Santiago, who did not return the gaze but nodded his head slightly. Then Carson and Kilmer, keeping their eyes on Longarm, walked over to the bar, where Ledger was filling the three shotglasses from an unlabeled brown bottle.

The Mexican remained in front of the door. His rain slicker was open to reveal the striped serape he wore beneath it, over a red calico blouse. His skin was Indian dark, and coal-black mustaches dangled down on either side of his narrow mouth. His forehead, beneath his black felt sombrero, which was banded with a javelina skin, bore three white slash marks above the bridge of his nose—likely some old gang insignia. He wore several pistols of various makes and calibers, and a very large Bowie knife with a beaded bone handle jutted from a sheath on his left thigh.

Carson took a filled shot glass off the bar and turned to face Longarm. Kilmer took one shot between his thumb and index finger and, holding it shoulder high, careful not to spill, walked over and gave it to Santiago, before turning and sauntering back to the bar. He picked up his own whiskey shot, tossed it back, and set the glass on the bar, wiping his little mouth above a weak chin with the back of his left hand, keeping the right one free for killing.

Santiago threw back half of his shot and studied the glass between his fingers, frowning disapprovingly. Carson threw back his shot and set the glass on the bar, then turned once more to Longarm, jerking his left thumb at Kilmer standing beside him. "Klute's got a bone to pick with you, Lawman."

"That's disturbing news," Longarm said, frowning at Kilmer.

"You done killed my cousin," Kilmer said. "Found him out there in the desert with his heart blown out. Layin' right there in the middle of the trail for the wild-cats to eat."

"And they was eatin', too," Carson said. "By the time we got to him, there was a mountain lion head-deep in ole Melvin's belly button."

Kilmer scowled indignantly at Carson. "Bill, you mind?"

The Mexican, Santiago, grinned, showing two gold eyeteeth. He kept his shiny black eyes on Longarm and was holding the whiskey shot chest-high before him as though he weren't sure what to do with it.

Kilmer whipped a glare at Longarm. "What you got to say for yourself, Lawman?"

Longarm turned his palms up on the table. "What could I possibly say that would ease your pain in this time of tragic loss?" He frowned. "Say, you fellas didn't happen to see two other lawdogs out there somewheres, did you? I was sort of expectin' to meet up with Ransom and Kitchen. In fact, I thought maybe you was them."

"Ransom and Kitchen, huh?" Carson drummed two fingers on his bottom lip, deep lines of feigned thought-fulness cutting into his forehead. "I don't know . . ." He let his voice trail off as he slid his eyes toward Kilmer.

The curly wolf from Tennessee walked over to Longarm's table, hauled the sack around in front of him, and set it on the table. "Ransom and Kitchen, huh?" he said, parroting Carson. He let the neck of the bag sag toward Longarm, picked up the bottom, and sort of shook it, until two human heads rolled onto the table in front of Longarm. "Could this be them?"

Longarm kept his expression stony as he glanced up from the heads, with their shocked, flat eyes and mouths opened in horror, to look at Kilmer without saying anything. His heart thudded, and his hands wanted to tremble, and he wanted more than anything to reach for his revolver just then.

But he waited.

Let one of them make the first move. That was how it was done. Even when the heads of two colleagues, men he had also considered friends, lay before him with their ragged bloody necks and faintly accusing eyes, flies buzzing around them.

Santiago snickered.

Carson, still at the bar, grinned delightedly.

Kilmer stretched a smile, showing crooked yellow teeth, and stepped back from the table, laughing and sticking his finger out jeeringly at Longarm. The lawman released the breath he hadn't realized he'd been holding.

They weren't going to draw on him, he saw. They were having too much fun. All three were laughing at him now, as though at the funniest joke they'd ever heard.

The fun, however, was over.

They hadn't expected it to be over so soon. Likely,

they'd figured he'd let them make the first play, which is really what he should have done, if he'd gone by the law. But he was outnumbered.

And the hacked-off heads of two good lawmen stared up at him from the table, the cheek of one nudging his speckled blue tin plate with the leavings of his stew on it.

And flames of fury lapped against his heart.

No, the fun was over.

And they weren't expecting it, he saw when he was able to drop his hands beneath the table and bring up both the double-action Colt and the double-barrel derringer faster than most men could blink. He used the Colt to shoot Carson first and triggered the derringer straight across the table at the Mexican laughing in front of the door.

Neither man had had time to do anything more than jerk with surprise before the slugs tore through him. Before the echoes of the two overlapping reports had died, Longarm stood up, hooked his arms beneath the table, and lifted it up, throwing it against Kilmer still standing before him, his Remington .44 half out of its holster.

The Remy crashed loudly, drilling a hole through the side of the table a quarter second before Longarm drove his shoulder against the underside of it and pushed the screaming Kilmer straight back toward the bar. The heads of the murdered lawmen flew, bounced, and rolled.

Before he reached the bar, Kilmer fell over a chair. Longarm slammed the table down on top of him, so that only the killer's face stuck out from one edge of it. Kilmer wore an expression similar to that of Ransom and Kitchen—shock and exasperation. Air exploded from his lungs when Longarm slid both his own knees up onto the table. He jumped up and down on the underside of it, causing air to blast out of the killer's lungs, his ugly face turning blue.

Longarm scuttled up closer to Kilmer's head, set his Colt down on the underside of the table, straightened his back, drew his right fist back behind his shoulder, and slung it straight down. It hammered the nub of Kilmer's cheek with a dull smack.

Kilmer squeezed his eyes closed and stretched his lips back from his teeth in horror.

Longarm drew his fist back again and flung it down once more. He drew it back and thrust it down again and again, going to work on the killer's cheeks and nose and chin until the man's screams had died and there wasn't much left of his face except for twenty or so deep gashes from which dark red blood oozed. His little, gray-yellow eyes stared straight up at Longarm from beneath swelling lids, slightly crossed and as sightless as those of the lawmen whose own heads lay nearby.

Longarm couldn't feel the man's chest rising and falling beneath the table. He lowered his fist, from which he'd scraped off most of the skin, and leaned forward on his hands and knees, raking air in and out of his tired lungs.

A silence had fallen over the station. Then a floorboard creaked to his right, just before Ralph Ledger cleared his throat behind the bar and said, "Uh . . . stage got in, Custis."

Longarm turned to his right. Six people of both sexes and varying ages stood to the left of the door, several feet away from the dead Ernesto Santiago. They stared in wide-eyed shock at Longarm, who was still down on all fours atop the table, beneath which lay the man he'd just beaten to death.

An old woman in a short traveling jacket, feathered hat, and gray skirt stood holding a suited boy of about ten in front of her, clamping her gloved hand over the youngster's eyes and regarding Longarm with bald disdain.

An old man stood beside her and the boy. There were also two gamblers and a young blond woman about Bella's age wearing a shiny green traveling frock and holding a carpetbag. She closed her open mouth and promptly passed out, one of the gawdy-suited gamblers catching her before she hit the floor.

Longarm heaved himself to his feet and stepped off the table still pinning Kilmer to the floor. He offered a weak smile and flexed his bloody-knuckled right hand. "Welcome to Hog's Head Station, pilgrims."

Chapter 6

Several hours later, after the bodies and the dead lawmen's heads had been hauled out of the station house and Ralph Ledger was scrubbing at a stubborn bloodstain on the barn near where Ben Carson had cashed in his chips, Longarm heard someone gasp.

He was sitting at a table near Ledger, sipping coffee laced with rye. He looked up to see the blond girl from the stage standing in the curtained doorway at the back of the room. Beyond the curtain lay the stage travelers' sleeping cribs. The girl stood poking her head and one shoulder out around the curtain, staring at Longarm with bald fear in her large, green eyes.

Ledger had heard the girl, too, and he stopped scrubbing to turn his head toward her. "Oh, now . . . it's all right, miss. All the bad men are done for. They just left a little blood behind's all."

He chuckled and sat back on his heels, wryly regarding the large stains on the floor fronting the bar. "Well, maybe a little more than a *little*. But they're gone, just the same. Harmless as jackrabbits. Me an' Longarm hauled 'em out in the desert and covered 'em up with rocks an' mud."

The girl kept her fear-bright eyes on Longarm. The light of the room's single lamp reflected in those clear, green orbs, so that they shone like gold in the sandy bed of a green mountain lake. Her throat worked as she swallowed. "Those . . . heads," she said softly, raspily, casting her gaze down at the floor near Longarm's boots, where the heads of the Ransom and Kitchen had fallen in the dustup.

Ledger glanced over his shoulder at Longarm with a pained expression.

Longarm slid his boots off the chair he'd propped them on. "Miss, would you like somethin' to eat? Coffee, mayhaps?"

She lifted her eyes again to Longarm, and they acquired that shiny, frightened cast, the corners deeply lined. Obviously, she figured him to be as down and nasty dirty as the men whose clocks he'd cleaned. The whole picture here in the station house had not been a pretty one. No wonder she was having trouble sleeping. The old woman had shuttled the little boy off to bed straightaway after entering and seeing the carnage, clucking her disdain at Longarm while holding both her hands over the shaver's eyes. The old man, loaded down with luggage, was close behind them.

The two gamblers whose names were Quinn and Dawson, were well accustomed to such violence, however.

They'd likely lived their entire lives on the seedy frontier. They'd stayed up and played a couple of games of cards while enjoying Ledger's whiskey before they, too, had shuffled off to the sleeping cribs, yawning and stretching and jingling the coins in their pockets, chuckling at the bloodstains on the station's scarred puncheon floors.

The girl merely stared at Longarm, not replying to his query.

Longarm rose from his chair, walked around to the water barrel that stood off the bar's far end, near the front wall, and removed the wooden lid. He took the tin cup hanging from a rusty nail above the barrel, dipped it into the barrel, then carried it dripping over to where the girl stood in the curtained doorway.

She shrank back from him a little, frowning up at him as he towered over her, but she kept her feet—which were bare, he saw—glued to the wooden floor. They were pale and delicate, the stubby toes pink as the rising sun and curled slightly against the wood. She held the curtain, shieldlike, before her.

"I've never seen the like . . ." she said, looking again toward Longarm's table.

"I am sorry you had to see that, miss." Longarm doffed his hat. "Name's Custis Long. I'm a deputy United States marshal, and I killed those men whose blood Mr. Ledger is scrubbing off the floor in the line of duty. They were bad, miss. Very bad. They killed the men—the U.S. marshals, friends of mine—who belonged to those heads." Longarm offered a weak smile. "But now they're tame as mice."

The girl studied him a moment longer, skeptically,

then reached out and grabbed the cup out of his hand. She wheeled, long, silky blond hair blowing out behind her, and disappeared into the sleeping quarters, from which several sets of snores issued.

The curtain jostled back into place behind her. Her smell lingered. It was not a fresh smell. After all, she'd likely been cooped up in the hot coach for days without a bath. But it was a tantalizing female smell, just the same. For a moment, it distracted Longarm from the knowledge that his two friends had been hideously butchered, and for that he quietly thanked her.

He'd buried the heads separately from the outlaws. But in this rain, which continued, though not as savagely as before, the burial of Ransom and Kitchen's remains had been done with little more ceremony than he'd used with Carson's bunch. He'd slopped some mud and rocks over them, touched a stiff finger to his hat brim, and hightailed it back to the barn with his shovel. He wasn't religious, and he doubted the dead marshals were, either.

He hadn't known what else to do with the heads. Such a grisly happenstance wasn't covered by government protocol—at least, none that he'd ever read about in the manuals—and he doubted that his boss, Chief Marshal Billy Vail, would want him to carry them back to Denver in a burlap croaker sack. Maybe in winter, but not here in the dog days of a blistering hot Wyoming summer. If he hauled them back to Billy, they'd be stinking to high heaven by the time he reached Denver.

Neither man was currently married, thank God, though he thought Ransom had a squaw somewhere down in New Mexico. Their not having wives to inform was about the only good thing in this situation Longarm could think of as he slacked back down in his chair and lifted his cup that was about half coffee and half badly needed whiskey.

"Here's to ya, gents," he muttered, raising the cup and giving his gaze to the front windows still beaded with the continuing rain, seeing lightning forking beyond them in the gray-black sky, hearing the resounding thunderclaps.

"What's that, Custis?" Ledger asked as he dunked his brush in the bucket of soapy water once more.

Longarm polished off the coffee and whiskey, set the cup down, and skidded his chair back from the table. "Said I'm headin' to bed."

He gained his feet a little unsteadily. Carson had been carrying in his saddlebags the money his and Dirty Jim's gang had stolen from the train. Longarm had taken possession of said bags, and now he lifted them from the back of his chair, tossed them over his left shoulder, and started for the door. "Sorry about the mess, Ralph."

"Ah, hell, Custis," Ledger said behind him. "I'm real sorry about your pards, that's all."

Longarm went out and found Bella Flowers asleep against the support post he'd tied her to. Old Jeff Thigpen and Hank Mitchum, the jehu who'd driven the stage last night, were snoring in the back lean-to room so loudly that Longarm could hear them even above the thunder and rain and the snorts of the fidgety horses.

The lawman double-checked Bella's stays. She slept with her head on her upraised knees, snoring very softly,

her chocolate curls hanging down her shoulders and
brushing the ground. He lowered the wick on the sole
burning lamp, dropped down against another support
post, the hay beneath him making a bed of sorts, and
vaguely heard himself begin snoring as he drifted asleep.

He woke to the first blush of dawn washing through
the barn's eastern windows, and to the grumbling of old
Jeff getting the team ready to be hitched to the coach
waiting outside. He hauled himself to his feet, splashed
some water on his face from a stock trough, ran his
hands through his wet hair, and donned his hat.

"Wake up, Sunshine!" he said, giving Bella's hip a
kick with his square-toed cavalry boot.

"Ow!" the girl grumbled, jerking her head up off her
knees but keeping her eyes squeezed shut. "Get away,
damn you." She lay her head back atop her knees, using
her hands for a pillow. "My day don't start till noon!"

That's pretty much how it went with the outlaw girl—
Longarm prodding her along while she cursed him
every step—until he had her outside the barn and crossing to the mud-splattered Concord sitting in the foot-
deep mud fronting the low-slung station house. Old Jeff
Thigpen and the driver, Hank Mitchum, were hitching
the team to the tongue while Ledger was stowing luggage in the boot and helping the passengers board the
coach. He'd formed a bridge of board planks from the
station house, so the passengers wouldn't have to wade
through the shin-deep muck.

"What—I'm ridin' in style to the hangman?" Bella
said snottily as Longarm led her along by an elbow.

"As far as the line goes, that is," Longarm told the

girl. He wanted to give the horses a rest, as they'd been through a lot and had a long, hot haul ahead of them. "Then we'll horseback the rest of the way to Moab. I'll send a telegram from the next Wells Fargo office, make sure the circuit judge is waitin' for us . . . with a fresh, green gallows just for you."

"Fuck you."

"Watch your tongue," Longarm said as the old woman, the old man, and the boy stepped out of the station house, the old woman scowling at the big lawman as she had the night before. Keeping his voice down, he added, "We're gonna be ridin' in polite society for a while, and I don't want you teachin' that child no new words or expressions. Understand?"

He saw her turn to him, sneering, and open her mouth to spout off again. He cut her off with: "One more nasty word, Miss Bella, and you'll be walkin' behind the stage with a rope around your neck."

She studied him. Seeing that he wasn't joking, she turned her mouth corners down and sighed in defeat.

When the old couple and the boy had boarded the coach, Longarm got Bella situated inside the carriage, as well. He put her on the rear seat facing forward and tied her cuffed hands to one of the half dozen leather handholds, in the form of loop-straps, dangling from the ceiling. It would make for an uncomfortable ride for the outlaw girl, but he didn't want her able to reach for his own or anyone else's sidearm. Besides, after what her gang had done to Ransom and Kitchen, she deserved more than a little discomfort.

To make sure she couldn't leap out of the stage and

run off, he tied her ankles together good and tight. The old couple and the boy watched in bald disdain of both the lawman and his prisoner. Longarm could see by her crossed eyes and pinched lips that Bella wanted to cuss him, but she bit her tongue, lips pursed, knowing he'd make good on his threat if she loosed any farm talk in front of the persnickety old woman and the boy.

When he had Bella trussed up as though for branding, he fetched his and her horses from the barn and tied them both to the rear of the coach. By the time he'd tossed their tack as well as his own rifle and the saddlebags containing the stolen train loot into the rear luggage boot, the gamblers had come out and boarded the stage. The only passenger who hadn't boarded yet was the blond girl.

"Fire your pistol in the air, Custis," said the driver, Hank Mitchum, who'd taken his seat in the driver's box and was itching to get going. "We're burnin' daylight!"

Longarm heard the door latch click and turned to see the girl step out onto the porch, carrying her carpetbag. She was dressed in the same tailor-made, snug-fitting traveling basque she'd been wearing last night. Her blond hair cascaded, lustrous with a recent brushing, down her delicate shoulders and across her small, pert breasts. Longarm walked over to the bottom of the porch steps and pinched his hat brim to the girl, trying to put her at ease. "Good mornin', miss. Lovely day, looks like. Can I take your bag?"

She clutched it to her bosom and glared at him haughtily. "Whatever for, you brigand?"

"Now, now," Longarm said. "I thought we got that

straightened out last night. I ain't an outlaw. I'm a law-man. And I do not intend to steal your bag, only to stow it in the boot for you."

"I'll take it, Custis," offered Ralph Ledger, brushing past him and meeting the girl at the top of the porch.

Longarm sighed and stepped back as Ledger took her bag, led her over to the coach, and helped her up the single step and inside. Longarm crawled in after her and squeezed into the seat between Bella and the door, find-ing himself directly facing the blond girl, who turned her head away from him coldly.

Ledger grinned as he closed and latched the door, shuttling his glance from Bella to the blonde then back again to Longarm. "Have a good trip, folks!"

He chuckled and stepped back.

Longarm glowered at him. "Just tell Hank to get us movin', Ralph," he said with a growl.

Chapter 7

For the first fifteen minutes of the ride out of Hog's Head Station, a tense silence hung like a dark cloud over the stage passengers. Trussed up as she was, leaning forward with her cuffed hands tied to the loop strap dangling from the ceiling in front of her, Bella was sort of like the five-hundred-pound ape in the carriage that everyone kept glancing at skeptically without saying anything.

Longarm figured it was probably pretty hard for the rest of them to reconcile such a beautiful girl and such treatment. The gamblers, the old man, the old woman, and the blonde, whose name Longarm had not yet learned, regarded him with brows arched in open rebuke. The little boy sat between the old couple across from Bella, staring openly at her, as though she were some alien creature that had dropped out of the sky. He'd probably never seen one of the fairer sex in such a situation, especially one as pretty as Bella.

For her part, the outlaw girl played up her torment
with the subtlety of an accomplished actress. She said
nothing but only leaned her head forward against her
cuffed wrists and squeezed her eyes closed as though
trying to sleep. Whenever the stage gave a violent rock
on its thoroughbraces, however, she groaned or grunted
and made an agonized face. A few times she glanced at
one of the gamblers or at the old couple with faintly beseeching eyes, then sighed raggedly, shifted her bound
ankles, turned her mouth corners down in defeat, and
leaned her head forward against her cuffed hands again.

Longarm chuffed out a breath and turned to look out
the window at the rocky, sage-stippled desert sliding
past, beyond the dust and occasional dirt clod or stone
kicked up by the galloping team.

The blonde was first to voice an objection.

She cleared her throat and said, just loudly enough
for Longarm to hear her above the shouts of the driver
and the clatter of the pitching carriage, "Say, there,
mister . . . don't you think you could loosen those a bit?"

Longarm turned to the girl, whose green eyes held
his with just a hint of hesitation as she leaned forward in
her seat and glanced at Bella sitting to the lawman's left.

"I do appreciate your concern, miss," Longarm said
with a casual smile. "As does Bella. But I'm not loosen-
ing anything on this killer sittin' beside me."

"Killer?" said the old woman, wrinkling her coarse,
ash-colored brows at Longarm before sliding her watery
blue gaze to the pathetic-looking brunette. "Surely not
this poor, frightened little thing!"

Longarm only pinched his hat brim at the old bat before returning his gaze to the Wyoming desert.

"The only one I saw doing any killing lately was you, sir." This from the blonde again, who leaned a little farther forward in her seat as she put some steel into both her eyes and her voice. "Never in my life, in fact, have I ever witnessed such savagery as that I was so unwillingly privy to last night at the Hog's Head station house!"

"Don't waste your breath," Bella said, looking at the blonde around her cuffed wrists. "He's just bound and determined to believe that I'm a hardened outlaw and career criminal." She gave a sob so authentic-sounding that even Longarm found himself half-believing it was real. "He just will not believe that I was taken off that train by those brigands, Dirty Jim and Ben Carson. Taken, you see, to help them in their getaway, and to be used . . ."

"There, there, now, miss," said the tallest of the two gamblers, sitting against the opposite stage wall from Longarm.

". . . in the most hideous ways imaginable!" cried Bella, pressing her head forward against her wrists and sobbing loudly, rocking her shoulders back and forth in fully feigned paroxysms of wretched despair.

The old woman gasped and closed her hands over the little boy's ears.

The old man sitting on the other side of the boy from the old woman flushed and blinked as he stared at the bawling Bella.

"Good Lord!" cried the blonde, directing her angry gaze at Longarm once more. "Can't you see she's . . .

she's grieving . . . ," she paused as though fumbling for words, ". . . the loss of her . . . her . . . *innocence*?"

"Bella never had no innocence," Longarm said dryly, growing not impatient but exasperated by the whole affair. "Even if she did have some at one point, she lost it a whole long time ago."

This made Bella bawl even more vehemently, as she ground her forehead against her wrists. Longarm chuffed and rolled his eyes.

"A lawman, you say?" This from the gambler sitting on the other side of Bella. He was a short, slender gent with a walrus mustache and a white-and-brown checked bowler hat. He regarded Longarm, blinking his brown eyes skeptically.

Longarm sighed, pulled his wallet out of his frock coat pocket, and flipped it open to reveal his badge. Everyone leaned forward or sideways to inspect the silver-chased tin, shuttling their gazes from the badge to Longarm as the stage rocked and swayed around them.

"The girl's a thieving liar and cold-blooded killer. She belongs to the gang that not only killed but *beheaded*"—he no longer cared what the boy heard or didn't hear—"two good lawmen and two good *friends* of mine. She tried to perforate my own hide yesterday morning—and would have if I hadn't emptied my pistol."

Longarm flipped his wallet closed and returned it to his coat pocket, barely keeping his temper on its leash. "Now, I'm taking her back to the federal jurisdiction in which she's wanted for robbery and murder, and I'd appreciated it if you'd all shut your rat traps and let me do it in peace!"

Bella twisted her torso around to face the gambler sitting to her right. "Thanks for trying, mister. You see, he's awfully stubborn, unwilling to listen to reason. I tried to get away from him yesterday—and paid the price for it. But no more. From now on, I'm just going to hope a jury believes my story of innocence and torment, and let the chips fall where they may."

She paused as she faced the two gamblers. Longarm could see only her back, but he knew she was letting both men get a good look at her deep cleavage inside her torn blouse, and the federal badge-toter gritted his teeth in vexation. "If we even make it back to Utah, that is. I mean, if he really is who he says he is and not just another one of those lustful road agent this country seems to be so teeming with."

With that last, she glanced sidelong and mockingly at Longarm over her shoulder.

He rolled his eyes and endured the glares of all inside the coach. The only one who wasn't looking at him as though he were the devil himself with tail curled and yellow fangs was the boy, who merely regarded him hopefully. Longarm smiled at the boy, trying to let him know he wasn't the ogre the others were making him out to be, but the boy only pursed his lips and beetled his little brows, kicking his legs, clad in shabby wool trousers with patched knees, against his seat.

Longarm had carried a federal badge longer than he cared to think about, and he'd tangled with nearly every brand of badman who'd ever ridden on the dusty frontier. But he'd never been in a situation like this: one in which he might be forced to defend himself against an old man, an old woman, a little boy, a beautiful young blonde with fiery green eyes, and two angry gamblers, lest they should all conspire to take his kill-crazy prisoner from him and turn her yapping mad on innocent citizens, including themselves!

Ignoring the stares and Bella's sympathy-evoking sobs, he returned his gaze to the desert. He dug a three-for-a-nickel cheroot out of the breast pocket of his coat, bit off the end with an angry snarl, spit it outside, and fired a match on his thumbnail.

He lit the cigar, blowing frustrated smoke puffs out the window but keeping one eye skinned on the gamblers. Only the taller one was wearing a Remington on his thigh, but the other could be harboring a hideout gun, as most gamblers did. He doubted either would try to shoot him in cold blood, but a fellow never knew what kind of high jinks a girl like Bella could provoke.

Especially when half of her delectable bosom was hanging out of her blouse and staring both men in the face!

Longarm was glad when Hank Mitchum pulled the coach to a stop atop a long hill and called, "Rest stop, ladies and gentlemen! Fifteen minutes!"

Longarm looked out the opposite side of the stage to see a rapids-ruffled stream twisting through cottonwoods at the base of a steep, chalky ridge. This would be Coffin Gap, he knew from frequent trails through the area. Even this late in the year the Coffin River would be cool with snowmelt shepherded down from the rocky ridges of the Continental Divide.

As the other passengers de-staged, continuing to re-gard Longarm like an old, nasty bear with his snout buried in a trash pile, the gamblers muttering to each other conspiratorially, the lawman reached up to cut Bella loose from the handhold dangling from the ceil-ing. They were alone in the stage now, the others head-ing off to tend to nature in the trees or drink from the stream. She saw it was safe to give him a devilish smile and a wink, and to say so close that he could feel her warm breath caress his earlobe, "The gamblers want to fuck me, Longarm. I have a feeling they're just desper-ate for it. Hope they don't do anything crazy!"

She chuckled throatily.

Longarm cut her ankles free then grabbed her cuffed hands and pulled her unceremoniously out of the stage. She gave an indignant shriek just loud enough for the others to hear. They all turned toward Longarm, as he half-dragged Bella around the back of the stage and behind the trailing saddle mounts toward a cottonwood, then looked at one another darkly, shaking their heads.

Longarm tied the outlaw girl's ankles together with rope from his saddlebags; then, leaving her sprawled in the shade of a large cottonwood, he took his canteen over to the stream and filled it. He could see the jehu, Mitchum, leading the team down to the stream to drink, well downstream from the passengers. To Longarm's left, the old woman was sitting on a rock while the old man filled a canteen at the stream. The little boy was walking around in the shady weeds among the trees, waving a stick gun around as though shooting Indians.

Both gamblers were on their hands and knees to his right. Their hats were off, and they were splashing water on their faces. The blonde knelt just beyond them, more carefully cupping water to her face and lips, trying not to get her muslin blouse wet.

Longarm held his canteen under the surface of the stream,which frothed over submerged rocks and boulders a few feet beyond the bank, and heard the water gurgle as it plunged down the flask's open mouth. Behind him, Bella beseeched everyone melodramatically: "Water? Oh, won't someone please bring me some water? He's tied me here, and I'm parched!"

Longarm chuckled as he lifted the canteen from the stream and shoved the cork in its mouth. He glanced at the others, the gamblers both standing now and staring toward Bella, their beards dripping.

"She'll live," Longarm said with a growl as he tramped through the weeds back to where the outlaw girl sat looking miserable, her hands cuffed and ankles tied, against the tree.

He dropped the canteen at her feet. "Your water, my queen."

She grinned covertly up at him and winked. "Thanks."

She lifted the flask with both her hands still cuffed, plucked the cork from the mouth, and held the canteen up above her head, letting the water run out onto her face, like a miniature waterfall. It flowed down her succulent lips and jaws and down her neck to soak her torn blouse. Longarm stared in mute male fascination as the water worked its magic on the cotton blouse, basting it tight as a second, see-through skin against her breasts.

But then he realized that the ploy was likely to fascinate the gamblers, as well. He grabbed the canteen out of her hands. "That'll be enough of that, you little prick-teaser."

Longarm hadn't realized that the gamblers had stolen up on him until he heard three gun hammers click behind him, one after the other. "That'll be enough of *you*, lawman!" the tall gambler said. "We're turnin' this poor little creature free, and we're doin' it right now!"

Chapter 8

Longarm turned to the two gamblers slowly moving up on him, their footsteps drowned by the stream's steady rush. The tall man held his Remington .36 in his beringed right fist, the hammer cocked, barrel aimed at Longarm's belly.

The other, shorter man—in a brown suit and paisley vest, with two steely little eyes and carefully trimmed muttonchop whiskers that swept out across his lower cheeks to connect with the ends of his waxed mustache—held two pearl-gripped derringers. He stood slightly to the left of the taller gent, his round spectacles winking in the sunlight filtering through the breeze-brushed cottonwood leaves.

The blond girl stood behind them, a few feet from the stream, facing toward Longarm and warily wringing her hands.

Longarm gave the pair of pasteboard artists a cold

look, curling half of his upper lip. "Put those hoglegs away, ya damn tinhorns. Before I take them away from you and shove them up your asses."

"Take that iron out of its holster," ordered the shorter gambler, stepping slowly toward Longarm and narrowing his little eyes behind his spectacles. "Real slow."

"You know how much time you'd do for interferin' with a federal marshal in the performance of his duties?"

"We don't believe you are a lawman, ya damn scoundrel," said the taller gent. "No bona fide badge-toter'd treat a poor, defenseless little girl like that so shabbily."

Bella, sitting against the tree with her breasts heaving behind her soaked blouse, sobbed.

The old woman and the old man flanked the gamblers about ten yards to the right of the blond girl. Both stared toward the commotion with shocked, stricken looks on their old, craggy faces.

"That won't save you from twenty years," Longarm said. "Hard labor."

"Bill done told you to drop that iron, mister." The tall man raised his cocked Remy, closing one eye as he stared down the barrel. "Throw it over here near me in the weeds . . . and any other gun you got tucked away somewheres."

Longarm studied both men, shuttling his enraged gaze from the cocked Remington to the two cocked, pearl-gripped derringers. Frustration sawed across his nerves like lightning dancing on a stony ridge. They had the drop on him. And by the hard, albeit witless, looks in their tinhorn eyes, they weren't fooling.

He glanced at Bella, who sat against the tree to his

right, her blouse pasted against her breasts. She looked up at him from beneath her brown brows, her eyes bright with mocking malevolence.

Longarm sighed. "You boys are sure makin' a mistake." Slowly, he snaked his right hand across his belly, unsnapped the keeper thong from over his Colt's barrel, and tossed the pistol into the grass near the tall gambler's brown shoes. "But it's your mistake, so I reckon you'll ride it out."

He held his hands up halfheartedly, fingers curled toward his palms.

The gamblers continued moving toward him.

"Better check him for a hideout!" Bella said with a snarl.

Both men looked at her, frowning.

"I mean . . ." She softened her voice, regaining her expression of a poor abused child. "I saw yesterday, when he was takin' a strap to me, that he carries a derringer in his right vest pocket. Better make sure he gives that up, too. I wouldn't want to see either of your merciful gentlemen injured on my account."

Longarm winced, resisting the urge to kick her in the chin.

"Give it up," said the little gambler, grinning.

"You boys are makin' a big mistake," Longarm repeated, slowly pulling the derringer out of its pocket, removing the gold-washed chain from the ring in the pearl butt, and tossing the gun into the weeds with his Colt.

The tall gambler turned to Bella. "He got anything else, miss?"

"I don't think so," she said weakly. "Please be care-

ful," she beseeched them, and Longarm was amazed at
how she could dribble so many tears down those pretty,
diabolical cheeks, and make them look real. "He's big
and mean, the scoundrel. I should know!"

Behind the gamblers and near the on-looking blonde,
the old woman gasped and covered her mouth with a hand.

Flushing with exasperation, the little gambler aimed
his two pocket pistols at Longarm's face and ordered
shrilly, "You take out your key and remove those cuffs
from that child! Put 'em on yourself and step back, ya
hear?"

The two gamblers were about ten yards away from
Longarm—far enough that he couldn't make a move on
them without taking a bullet. Likely several. So, with
another fateful sigh, he removed the handcuff key from
his pocket, crouched down, and, holding Bella's subtly
mocking gaze with a threatening one of his own, un-
locked the handcuffs.

"Oh!" she cried when the cuffs came away from her
wrists, clutching her hands to her breasts that were nearly
fully revealed behind her soaked blouse. As Longarm
sawed with his pocketknife through the ropes tying her
ankles, she squeezed her wrists as though the pain of
the blood running back into her hands was unendurable.

Longarm chuckled as he straightened, regarding the
two gamblers grimly. "She's free now," he said, giving
his level gaze to the two gun-wielders. "You just best
make sure she don't get her hands on a gun."

Suddenly, Bella lowered her wrists and raised her head,
chuckling and kicking the cut rope away from her ankles. She stood, lowering her arms to reveal her breasts

behind the clinging blouse, and glanced at the two gamblers as she walked past them toward the creek. "Thanks, fellas."

"Hey," the tall gambler said, turning his head to follow her with his eyes, "where you goin', miss?"

She continued walking back toward the blonde, who'd moved up a ways from the creek. Bella swung her hips enticingly, taking long strides. She crouched to pluck Longarm's Colt out of the brush and dust it off.

"I told ya," Longarm muttered. "That there's the one thing you *don't* wanna let her do."

The gamblers stared at her lustily, only vaguely perplexed. The girl's breasts bouncing around behind the wet blouse had them glamored, their feet glued to the ground as they stared at her.

"Like I said," Bella said, ratcheting back the hammer of Longarm's Colt to full cock. "I do appreciate it."

She extended the pistol at the tall gambler and promptly shot him through the head. He had not yet fallen like a tall tree sawed down in the forest before she'd drilled a second pill through the little gambler's face, just below his left eye.

The little man's head jerked back, and he lost his glasses as he staggered and fell.

Laughing, Bella turned the gun on Longarm. She didn't quite get it aimed at his head before the gun dropped suddenly out of her hands, hit the ground with a thud.

Longarm had been staring at the gun. Now, as the crack of a rifle flatted out over the valley from somewhere behind him, he raised his gaze to Bella and saw the quarter-sized hole in the girl's forehead and the blood and white bone and brain matter spraying out the back of her skull toward the blonde standing about six feet directly behind her.

Bella stumbled back, lowering her hands as if to break her fall, though they did no such thing, for she was dead before she hit the ground.

She fell with her head on the feet of the blonde, who stared down at her, her face crimson behind her white hands, which she'd clamped over her mouth as though to stifle a scream. The old woman's eyes rolled back into her head. She began to fall off the rock she'd been sitting on, but the old man hurried to grab her and ease her onto the ground at the base of the boulder.

Longarm whipped his gaze back toward the slope rising on the other side of the teamless stage. Hank Mitchum ran toward him from downstream, the burly driver's face a mask of incredulity as he regarded Bella still lying at the shocked blonde's feet with her brains blown out, and then the dead gamblers.

"Holy shit!" the driver cried. "What in God's name is goin' on here, Custis?"

"Stay with the passengers, Hank!"

Longarm ran forward, appraising the slope beyond the trail with his keen-eyed gaze but spying no shooter. He reached into the stage's rear boot, slid his Winchester out of its leather sheath, pumped a cartridge into the chamber, then ran across the trail and up the rocky slope at an angle. There were tufts of tawny grass and a few piñons and cedars, but mostly rocks and clay-colored gravel.

As he ran, he swept the slope with his eyes, trying to catch some sign of the shooter. He'd been somewhere on the slope, because here was the only place he could have been to have made that shot, and the slope was where the report had sounded from. Longarm was twenty feet from the ridge crest, breathing hard, when something caught his eye to his right.

He stopped, crouched, and picked up the .56-caliber cartridge casing between his right thumb and index finger. It was still warm, and the open end smelled like burned cordite.

He pocketed the casing, spied a boot print in the gravel near where he'd found it, then continued running up and over the crest of the ridge. Ten feet down from the top, he stopped where he wouldn't be skylined, and dropped to a knee. He looked across a broad gulley then quickly raised his rifle to his shoulder, thumbing back the hammer.

A rangy rider on a mouse-brown dun was lunging up the opposite slope at a steep angle. The man wore a red-and-black checked shirt, a green bandanna, and a broad-brimmed, tan Stetson. The sheathed rifle lashed to the saddle over the horse's right hip flopped as the horse ground its front hooves into the gravel and pushed off its hindquarters. The rider crouched low over the saddle-horn, elbows high, batting his black boots against the horse's flanks.

Longarm laid the Winchester's sites on the man, whose face he could not see from this vantage point, and while he felt no real anger toward the man who'd saved his life by drilling Bella, he squeezed the trigger.

The rifle leaped and roared. It was only a vague attempt. Dust puffed from the side of the slope, about two feet right of the horse and rider, as the grulla bounded to the top of the ridge then plunged from sight.

Longarm ejected the spent shell casing and levered a fresh one into the chamber. He studied the ridge over which the rider had disappeared. The man's dust wafted in the mid-morning sunlight.

The man had saved his life, but something told Longarm it hadn't been intentional. He'd been out to shoot Bella. Or maybe he'd been trying to shoot Longarm—God knew how many enemies the federal lawman had gunning for him—but botched the job and killed Bella instead.

Or . . . maybe he'd been after the stage itself, believing wrongly that it was hauling a strongbox. Of course he might have been after the loot from the mail train, but how would anyone know Longarm was carrying it?

Baffled, he walked up to the crest of the ridge and glanced back toward where the coach waited on the trail near the cottonwoods and the stream. Even from this distance he could plainly see there was nothing—not even any luggage—strapped to the coach's roof. Strongboxes were rarely carried in the rear luggage boot.

Could the killer, then, have been after the loot? Could he be a seventh member of Dirty Jim and Ben Carson's bunch—one who hadn't taken part in the robbery itself but was now out for the stolen loot?

Longarm's head swam so that the ground pitched and swayed around him. He stood a little wobbly on his feet and rested his rifle on his shoulder. He looked toward where the ambusher had vanished; then he dropped down the ridge and made his way back to the stagecoach. The horses were cropping grass in the trees. The old woman was still sitting back against the boulder, with the old man down on one knee beside her, fanning her stricken-looking face with his hat. The boy knelt in the grass near the stream, staring toward Bella and the two dead gamblers, both still lying where they'd fallen.

Longarm couldn't see the blonde.

Mitchum sat on a rock near where the short gambler lay on his side in the grass. The jehu was leaning forward with his elbows on his knees, smoking a cigarette. As Longarm came up, he turned and thumbed a tobacco flake from his tongue, brushed it on his patched, baggy duck trousers. "Fine mess, Custis. Mighty fine. How's a driver s'posed to keep a timetable with you around?"

Chapter 9

"I didn't fire a damn shot, Hank," the big lawman said, walking past the dead gamblers to where Bella lay dead in the grass. "Leastways, not at any of these folks. The one I did fire, at the hombre who cleaned my prisoner's clock, sailed wide."

Mitchum stood up and looked at the dead gamblers as he thumbed his suspenders out from his broad chest and bulging belly. He took a drag from his quirley and blew the smoke out his sun-leathered nostrils. "How do you account for it?"

"Which part of it?"

"Who shot the gamblers?"

"Bella did."

"Who shot Bella?"

Longarm plucked the cartridge he'd found on the ridge from his pants pocket and squinted at it. "Some hombre with a big fuckin' gun. A Spencer .56 is my guess."

"Why?"

"Why what?" Longarm was owly. He couldn't answer that question for himself, much less for the old jehu.

"Why'd he shoot your prisoner?"

"Quit askin' so damn many questions," Longarm growled as he leaned down and picked Bella up in his arms. Odd to see her suddenly so lifeless when she'd been not only so full of life just a few minutes ago, but about to take his. "Help me get these bodies over to the stage. We'll haul 'em to the next relay station, bury 'em there."

As he carried Bella toward the stage, he glanced back at Mitchum. "Where's the blonde?"

"Miss Hunter?" Mitchum pinched his quirley out with his thumb and index finger. "Think I seen her head back this way," he said, jerking his head upstream.

When Longarm and Mitchum had gotten the two dead men and Bella hoisted up to the stage roof, Mitchum fetched the old man, the old woman, and the boy, while Longarm walked through the breeze-jostled cottonwoods, looking for Miss Hunter.

He found her sitting on a downed tree trunk about fifty yards from the stage. She faced away from him, back straight, hands resting on her thighs.

Longarm walked around the crown of the tree that still had most of its branches and leaves—a recent blowdown, most likely—and approached the girl from the side. She did not look at him but only stared straight upstream through the cottonwoods and pines, expressionless, not moving, as though she were made of stone.

"Miss Hunter?"

She said nothing, did nothing to indicate that she'd heard him.

Longarm stayed about fifteen yards away from her and to one side, facing the stream. She stared straight ahead of her into the trees in which a squirrel was chittering and the breeze was rustling the leaves. "You all right, miss?"

He waited.

After nearly a minute, she said thinly, "I . . . want to go home."

She did not appear to be crying. Her face, her eyes, remained stony, her back straight.

"Where you from?"

"Homerville, Minnesota."

"What brings you out this way?"

She turned her head to him slowly, as though she were still half in a trance. "Are you really a lawman?"

"That's right."

"She killed those gamblers after they freed her." Miss Hunter wrinkled the skin above the bridge of her nose. "Why . . . did she . . . do that?"

"Because she was bad."

This didn't seem to satisfy the blonde. She sat regarding Longarm blankly, as though she were waiting for him to explain it to her more fully.

"We'd best get back on the stage, Miss Hunter."

"How do you know my name?"

"Mitchum told me." Longarm offered a friendly smile. "He didn't tell me your first name, though."

She swallowed and turned her head forward again. "I don't want to get back in that smelly thing. I'm sick of the dust, and I'm sick of the smells and the rocking and"—her voice acquired a slight quaver—"all this bloody *murder.*"

For some reason, just then it occurred to Longarm that since Miss Hunter had been standing directly behind Bella when Bella was shot, perhaps Bella's bullet had been meant for her. He studied her clean-lined profile. He could see her right green eye. Her skin was the color of a ripe peach and smooth as varnished pine. Her honey-blond hair fell down over her shoulder, rich as ripe wheat.

No one could want to kill her. Hell, she was from Minnesota, for chrissakes. No one ever wanted to kill anyone from Minnesota, least of all a pretty, green-eyed girl who'd likely never so much as kicked a pesky cat out off her piano bench.

"Don't blame you a bit, Miss Hunter. I'm sure we can arrange to send you back to Minnesota . . . just as soon as we get you to the next relay station. There'll probably be another stage heading back toward where you came from soon. After all you been through, I'll make sure it don't cost you a penny."

Of course, he didn't know if Billy Vail would go for it, but Longarm would pay for the girl's return trip home out of his own pocket if necessary. She looked so shocked and lost and heartbroken, sitting there. He felt guilty for his part, however unpreventable, in terrifying her.

"Did you shoot . . . her . . . ?"

From where she'd been standing, and in the state she'd likely been in after Bella shot the gamblers, she probably hadn't seen where the shot that killed Bella had come from.

"No, I didn't," Longarm said gently, extending his hand to the girl. "Come on now, Miss Hunter. Let's get you aboard the stage and on to the next relay station. You could do with some food and good hot coffee to clear the cobwebs. I could use some my ownself."

She sighed and rose from the tree, brushing bits of bark from the back of her traveling dress. Ignoring Longarm's proffered hand, she walked past him and on back toward the waiting coach, to which the driver was just now finishing hitching the team.

As Longarm approached the coach, six feet behind the girl, the old couple's little boy poked his head and arm out the window, making a gun with his thumb and index finger.

"Bang! Bang! Bang!" he cried in wild-eyed glee. "You're *dead*!"

Miss Hunter gasped and wheeled and threw her arms around Longarm's neck and pressed her face to his chest.

"Jubal, you stop that this instant!" intoned the old woman from inside the carriage. She grabbed the waistband of the boy's pants and hauled him back inside the coach.

Miss Hunter shook in Longarm's arms.

"Now, now," Longarm said, rubbing his hand across her slender, shuddering back. "It's just the boy havin' a little fun—that's all."

She pulled her head away and looked up at him in chagrin, flushing. Finally, she released him and stepped back in embarrassment. "Sorry," she said, sliding a wing of thick, blond hair back away from her crimson cheek but not meeting his gaze. "I guess my nerves are a little shot."

"I know just how you feel."

He did, too.

He helped her up into the stage; then, wanting to keep a lookout for a possible return of the bushwhacker, he climbed into the driver's box with Hank Mitchum. The jehu himself had already taken his place and was drinking from his canteen.

There being no shotgun rider, there was plenty of room on the sun-silvered and badly splintered driver's seat. Longarm stowed his rifle in the boot beneath it, where Mitchum kept his shotgun, and glanced back at the two dead gamblers and the dead girl on the roof behind him. He'd tied the bodies to the brass rails that ran around the edge of the roof, so they couldn't roll off.

The gamblers lay with their feet toward Longarm. Bella lay with her head toward him, her body sort of angled across the roof to the left of the tallest sharpie. Blood had pooled beneath her head. Her eyes were open and staring beneath the puckered, quarter-sized hole in her forehead. Her hands lay limp on the coach roof to either side of her.

She was a killer without dispute, and she'd had that

bullet coming. Still, Longarm remembered the night he'd lain with her—before she'd tried to kill him—and he couldn't help feeling a pang of regret that she was dead—a pretty girl, a wasted life.

"Time to roll, folks!" Mitchum shouted as he shoved the brake handle forward with a moody curse, releasing the wooden blocks from the wheels.

Longarm turned to the front and wedged his boots against the dashboard for support as the jehu hoorahed the rested team on up the trail.

The trace wound through the fragrant pines at the top of the pass before dropping down into a little valley. As they were climbing into the cool slopes of the Wind River Mountains, ominous purple clouds with dramatically scalloped edges appeared, capping the next high western peak. Holding his hat down snug on his head, his string tied whipping over his shoulder, Longarm stared at the threatening mass.

It grew larger as it moved toward him, shepherded by a fresh, cool breeze. Distant thunder rumbled, and the spruces and tamaracks jutting around him grew darker as the sun was quickly swallowed, and the light faded to a charcoal-gray.

"Holy shit," Mitchum said, pulling his own battered sombrero down lower on his nearly bald skull. "Looks like we're about to be gettin' another taste of the summer monsoon!"

He muttered to himself in disgust then shook the reins over the team's pitching backs, urging more speed. "We gotta get beyond the East Fork of Hell Creek before it floods, or we could be stranded out here for days!"

They crossed the wooden bridge over the currently placid creek of concern just in time. The rear wheels had no sooner rattled off the gray wooden boards than thunder boomed like God hammering a giant war drum just above the tops of the bending pines. Rain came slashing straight down at first from the low, gray sky— raindrops as large as wheel hubs and instantly making puddles in the trail's numerous chuckholes.

Longarm and the driver were soaked within seconds, the rain sluicing off their hats. Fortunately, the Stage Relay Station was only another ten minutes up the trail, and they dropped down into it from over a low pass. The yard was a sea of gray mud pelted by the driving rain. The two half-breed Cheyenne women who ran the place, Loueen and Virginia Ten Horses, hustled with open umbrellas out of the two-story cabin, which was fronted by a brush-roofed gallery. They were both dressed as white women, in crisp gingham with aprons, their long, black hair braids hanging down their backs.

As they sheltered the old woman and Miss Hunter into the station house, Longarm helped Mitchum and Virginia's son, Clifford Chief's Bear, who was the station's sole hostler, unhitch the team and lead it into the barn across the yard from the cabin. Mitchum and the tall, beefy Indian youth, dressed in the garb of a white cowpuncher, tended the team. Longarm smoked a cigar between the barn's open doors, watching the gray curtain of rain buffeted by the wind before him.

The coach's wheels had sunk a good foot in the mud. The bodies on its roof lay still as dozing nappers as the

rain washed them clean of blood and guts if not their
sins . . .

He looked east of the muddy yard, toward the low
pass they'd just crossed but which he could barely see
through the storm. Vaguely, he expected to see the bushwhacker sitting there in his red-and-black checked shirt
and broad-brimmed hat, a big-model rifle resting butt-
down on his thigh—watching, waiting for another shot.

At whom?

At Longarm himself?

Or had he already done the job he'd set out to do, and
was he a long ways away from here?

Longarm drew a lungful of the pungent but invigo-
rating cigar smoke and blew it into the rain as he returned his gaze to the storm-battered stage. "Who killed
you, Bella?"

Chapter 10

The rain continued, flooding the creeks and preventing the stage from continued travel at least until the morning.

The one good thing was it gave Longarm plenty of time to bury his party's three most recent corpses, which he did during a half-hour lull in the storm, putting the three to rest in separate graves on a low, wet, grassy hill south of the station.

Possibly friends or family might want the bodies moved, but they'd have to come fetch them themselves. Or the stage company could move them. For now, Longarm just wanted them out of the way.

He had more important things to think about—like Bella's killer, for instance. And getting the stolen train loot back to Utah. He kept a sharp eye skinned for the bushwhacker while he dug the graves with a pick and a spade, not bothering with going too deep and merely rolling the bodies up in their own bedrolls, filling in the graves, and piling a few rocks on each muddy mound.

He wasn't a gravedigger but a lawman. And he never much stood on ceremony.

Old Mitchum hadn't offered to help, though the gamblers had been his passengers. Even Bella had been his charge, if you wanted to get down to brass tacks, since Longarm had paid the company Uncle Sam's money for passage. But the old jehu had sought refuge inside the station, drinking the Ten Horses sisters' home-brewed beer and forty-rod for which they were locally famous and which had turned into a considerable sideline, though they never drank the stuff themselves.

He didn't hold it against the oldster. When he was finished with the grisly chore, he returned the shovel to the barn then joined the jehu on the front gallery. The Ten Horses sisters served them antelope stew with wild onions and potatoes from their garden, as well as their special busthead. Eating and then relaxing and drinking and smoking, Longarm and the old driver, who'd been many things before he'd started working for stage companies, talked about the old days, meaning the days just after the War, when they'd both headed west, and after the hide-hunting days, when they'd headed farther west, and had run into each other from time to time.

All in all, there weren't that many folks in the vast West, so you tended to be friendly with those you met, and Longarm figured he'd known old Hank Mitchum for twenty years or longer. He wouldn't really call the man a friend—he suspected the jehu of riding the outlaw trail a time or two in his rich and varied past—but a friendly acquaintance. Just the same, he enjoyed palavering with the old-timer while smoking and drinking and whiling away this stormy afternoon.

The bushwhacker had for all intents and purposes ended his current mission, after all. He had only to return the train loot to the Utah jurisdiction from which it had been stolen—he could do that via Wells Fargo strongbox from Laramie on his way back to Colorado—and then return to Denver, where Chief Marshal Billy Vail would doubtless hit him with a new assignment.

For now, he could cool his heels.

But he couldn't completely let his guard down.

Although he was kicked back in his chair and enjoying the rain and his whiskey and cigars, and the low, raspy, wandering rhythms of Mitchum's woolgathering monologue, tension pricked at the edges of the lawman's consciousness, like a mouse chewing at the underside of a cabin floor.

That damn bushwhacker.

Longarm's job was not done. It had just gained another component. He had to run the killer down. The drygulcher might have killed a killer, but he was a killer himself. He'd face a jury and likely a hangman's rope just the same as if he'd shotgunned a parson on a golden Easter morning.

Mid-afternoon, Mitchum headed up to the cabin's second story, where crudely furnished but comfortable rooms were maintained for passengers, to take a nap. Longarm remained in the chair he was beginning to grow into, a tin coffee cup, kept filled and properly spiced by one of the Ten Horse women, steaming on the

rail before him, his rifle resting across his knees as a
security blanket of sorts.

About an hour after Mitchum left, the cabin door
creaked open, and Miss Hunter walked out onto the
gallery. She looked rested, her hair freshly brushed.
Minnesotans must spend a lot of time on their hair,
Longarm idly opined to himself. He studied the pretty
blonde as she closed the door, looked out at the rain that
had slowed to a steady drizzle dropping from a sky the
color of greasy rags, then walked over and sat down in
the chair that Mitchum had vacated. She held a blanket
about her shoulders against the rainy, high-country chill.

She had a mysterious, pensive look about her. Not
friendly but not unfriendly. She said nothing for a time,
but Longarm suspected she was building up to something. He kept his mouth shut so as not to intrude upon
her thoughts.

"I had always heard that the fragrance of mountain
air was worth making the trip west for all by itself," she
said, sitting straight-backed at the edge of her chair and
staring across the yard toward the barn and the green-
forested slope rising behind it.

She lifted her nose, taking a deep breath.

"So, what's your conclusion?" Longarm said.

"It was."

"Now you're ready to go back home?"

"No."

The response surprised him. She shook her head
slowly as she continued to stare across the yard and beyond the barn that was a large, brown splotch in the
grayness. "I am going to continue my journey to its end,

and stay as I was planning to stay all along. I had heard the West was a wild and often vile place. So I knew what I was getting into. I just hadn't realized I'd get into it so quickly."

She shook her head again and pursed her lips, her green eyes resolute. "No, I will continue on as planned.

Longarm had taken another sip of his coffee, and now, hearing the girl's intended destination, he choked a little as he swallowed and chuffed ironically at the same time. He scowled at her and said with his windpipe still pinched, "Hell Creek?"

"That's right." Miss Hunter smiled for the first time in his presence, but he was too perplexed to fully appreciate that it was a right pretty smile. "Hell Creek." She said it as though enjoying the crisp way it rolled off her pink lips.

"Pardon me for bein' so forward, Miss Hunter, but do you know where Hell Creek is, exactly?"

"Of course I do. I was sent a map along with the deed to my uncle Lester's Hell Creek Ranch." She extended her arm and one long, pale finger toward the southwest, over an especially tall, forested ridge partly hidden by gauzy, low-hanging clouds. "It's that way. Twenty miles or more."

"No, twenty miles is about right. But it's up high and out in the middle of nowhere. The only folks who live there are outlaws, former outlaws, prospectors, and coyotes. I don't even think the stage goes there!"

"It does when someone books passage to Hell Creek. We'll be swinging up that way tomorrow, I'm sure."

Longarm sucked on his cigar and pondered all that.

The last time he'd been through Hell Creek, which sat on the shoulder of Hell Mountain on the southern slopes of the Wyoming Range, was on the trail of several outlaws that had holed up there, because there'd been no law in Hell Creek. He doubted there was any law there still, but likely plenty of curly wolves.

No, Hell Creek was no place for a pretty, innocent girl from Minnesota.

He blew out a long smoke plume into the drizzle beyond the gallery's eave, took another drink from his wonderfully spiced, hot, black belly wash, and, so fortified, scowled at the girl once more. "What'd you say your business is up there on that canker on the devil's . . . uh . . . I mean, backside?"

"My Uncle Lester Debo died last spring. He willed me his ranch. My family—Pa, Ma, my sister Sue and brother Ed—all died in a cyclone last fall. The twister whipped through our farmstead outside of Homerville and swept them all up in it. Threw 'em down pretty near a mile away. I was off selling eggs at the Wilbur farm, or I'd be gone, too."

She turned to Longarm with shiny eyes, a single tear rolling down along the side of her nose. "I have no one, you see? And I have nothing . . . except Uncle Lester's ranch."

"I am sorry for the tragedy that's befallen you, Miss Hunter. But your Uncle Lester's ranch might as well be on the backside of the moon. I doubt there's any folks left in Hell Creek since the gold pinched out of the mines up there. You'll likely be all alone! And . . . have you ever run a *ranch* before?"

"Well, I've run a farm. Pa was a good man . . . when he wasn't drunk. I'm afraid my brother wasn't the farming sort, either, so most of the work was left up to me, Ma, and Sue. We got the crops in, and we harvested them, ran a few head of beef, and had a whole flock of barred rocks running around our yard, laying the best eggs you've ever seen fried sunny side up. We did all that, and even managed to get schooling in. Ma had been a teacher before she met Pa. She taught us how to read and write and figure, so we would be beholdin' to no one."

Miss Hunter looked off and hiked a shoulder, wringing her pale hands nervously in her lap. "If push comes to shove, I figure I can probably teach if the ranching isn't so good at that altitude."

"I doubt there's anyone who needs learnin' up that high, Miss Hunter." Longarm shook his head and narrowed his eye at the girl. "How old are you?"

"Twenty-two."

He studied her thoughtfully. He'd have thought she was a little younger, for there was indeed a tender, country-style innocence about her. But her eyes owned a mature stubbornness. And from what little he could see of her figure behind the bulky traveling outfit and the blanket she held about her shoulders, she was tricked out with all the angles and curves of a well-set-up woman.

"Well," Longarm said, leaning back in his creaky chair, "I reckon you're old enough to make your own decisions. But I strongly advise you to go on back to Homerville, Miss Hunter. Surely there's more for you there—friends, maybe a boy you could marry up with— than there is in Hell Creek, Wyoming."

"Rest assured, I do not intend to marry some worthless cad."

The restrained anger with which she'd made the proclamation caused Longarm to give her a sidelong glance, one brow arched. She sat her chair, straight-backed and prim, staring resolutely and hard-eyed beyond the barn and over the ridge toward her place of destination.

Without bothering to explain the exclamation, she rose from her chair and said, "I've offered the Ten Horses sisters my help with supper, so I'll be taking my leave now, Marshal."

"Call me Longarm."

She glanced over her shoulder at him. "All right, then. I reckon it wouldn't be improper, since we're traveling together and all, for you to call me Sarah."

She turned away from him curtly and went on inside the station house where the Ten Horses sisters were knocking pans and stove lids around as they started preparing the evening meal.

It stopped raining mid-evening, and the night was clear. Longarm had a last cigar out on the gallery, enjoying the freshness of the storm-cleansed air, then took a walk around the yard's perimeter.

Spying no one suspicious on the lurk, he fetched his saddlebags from the stage's boot, as well as the bags containing the stolen train loot, and his rifle, and hauled the gear upstairs to one of the cots partitioned off by Indian blankets hanging from ropes. There were four similarly partitioned cribs on each side of the attic. The old man and the old woman occupied two, while the little boy occupied another. Both the old folks' snores resounded off the steeply angled, pine-paneled walls.

Longarm saw an open crib on the hall's right side, at its far end, and went in and set his gear quietly down on the floor and atop the single Windsor chair that the eight- by six-foot niche was furnished with. He stripped down to his summer-weight balbriggans, splashed water from the washbowl over his face and head and behind his neck, toweled off, then crawled beneath the freshly starched sheet and the quilt and set his head back on the surprisingly comfortable pillow.

He released a deep breath and closed his eyes.

The sound of gently splashing water came from behind the blanket to his left. He could hear someone breathing over there. There was a jagged tear in the blanket partitioning his crib off from the one on that side of him. Natural male prurience caused him to close one eye and with the other peer through the ragged gash.

Enough milky moonlight angled through the window of the next crib for him to see Sarah Hunter standing on the other side of the blanket, in front of her washstand. He couldn't see much of her through the jagged-edged slit—only one slender arm and the entire side of a naked breast.

In the moonlight, the breast was full and creamy and tipped with a budlike nipple, and it shifted enticingly as she ran a wet sponge slowly, luxuriously across it.

She was breathing slowly, deeply, taking her time with the washing, enjoying herself, pleasuring herself,

cupping her breasts in her hands, squeezing them, looking down at them. She slid her thumbs back and forth
across her nipples, lifted her chin, closed her eyes, drew
a deep breath and released it with a long sigh and a thin,
raspy moan.

Longarm's cheeks warmed with shame. He told himself to turn away. This was the girl's time alone. He was
a wretched cur for invading her privacy. But his neck
had turned to stone. He could not move his head.

The water tinkled quietly as the girl continued to
slowly run the sponge across her breasts, with one hand
while squeezing and the other kneading them. She kept
her chin raised toward the ceiling, her blond hair cas-
cading down her arched, shadowed back. The sides of
her hair shone like silver in the moonlight. Her shoulders rose and fell deeply as she gave occasional, barely
audible moans and groans.

She gasped. One arm jerked up to cover her breasts
as she turned toward Longarm.

The lawman's heart thudded. He jerked his head back
down on his pillow. He heard the curtain slide back on
its rope.

He squeezed his eyes closed and feigned a snore. The
girl's eyes burned into him. Inwardly, he winced, but he
continued to rake snores across his tonsils, blowing
them out across his pooched lips.

"Are . . . are you awake?" she whispered tensely.

Longarm snored again, hoping he wasn't overdoing
it. He heard her breathing, watching, waiting only two
feet away.

Finally, he heard the curtain slide back into place, and his heartbeat slowed.

The recent image of her fondling herself had burned itself in his brain, however, and it took a long time for him to tumble off into untroubled sleep.

Chapter 11

Longarm woke with a hard-on the next morning, the residue from frenzied sex dreams of pink-nippled breasts enmeshed in long, silky, honey-blond hair mashing themselves against his face. He gave his cock a whack on the edge of his cot, rose, and dressed.

Judging by the blankets still in place across their crib doors, Sarah Hunter and the other three passengers were still asleep. They would probably sleep for another hour. Through an east-facing window at the rear of the attic, Longarm could see that the sky was still dark, though the night was slowly lightening toward lilac.

The lawman went downstairs. Mitchum was up, having coffee with Clifford Chief's Bear, while the youth's mother and aunt were, respectively, peeling potatoes and cutting bacon from a cured pig belly. A fresh stack of split wood stood near the kitchen's large, black, ticking range—the predawn work of Clifford, most likely.

Loueen Ten Horses presented Longarm with his own mug of steaming java so black it could have floated a wheel hub, and he sat and gassed with Mitchum and Clifford while he waited for breakfast. Nearly an hour later, the passengers were up and fed, and when Clifford had hitched a fresh team to the stage, Mitchum poked his head in the cabin's front door and hollered, "All aboard, folks. Next stop, Hell Creek . . . if we can make it, that is."

"What do you mean, if we can make it?" asked Sarah Hunter as the others filed off the gallery ahead of her.

"Steep trail up there, miss. Might have washed out. We'll see, though . . ."

Longarm was outside, tying his bay and the black horse he'd inherited from Bella to the rear of the coach. He'd decided over breakfast that he'd continue west with the stage for at least another day, in case the bush-whacker who'd killed Bella showed himself again. Also, he was not completely convinced the killer hadn't been out to drill Sarah. It was unlikely that the blonde from Minnesota could have angered anyone enough to put a bullet through her head, but the lawman felt compelled to make sure.

If the drygulcher really had been out to kill Bella, Longarm would likely never see him again. He couldn't track him, as his trail would have been obliterated by the recent bad weather. But if the killer was after Long-arm himself, or the loot, or the girl, he would probably see him again soon.

At any rate, he was in no hurry to get back to Denver. It was hot down there on the eastern Colorado plains.

Cooler up here. Prettier, too, he thought now as he watched Mitchum help Sarah Hunter board the stage, remembering last night with a passing twinge of shame.

And he wanted to run that bushwhacking killer to ground.

When all the passengers were aboard the stage, and Longarm had stowed the loot and the rest of his gear in the rear boot, he climbed aboard and sat in the driver's box beside Mitchum, laying his loaded Winchester across his thighs. As the jehu hoorahed the team on out of the muddy yard and along the gradual grade toward the next pass, Longarm raked his gaze through the forest pushing up close on both sides of the meandering, rocky trail.

The sun had just risen in the clear sky, and heavy shadows lingered in the fragrant pinewoods. Longarm smelled balsam and pine resin and the heavy fragrance of deep forest duff. Squirrels chattered and magpies squawked. Robins flitted among the branches that glistened, beaded in golden raindrops, as the sun's strengthening rays hit them.

All the usual sights and sounds and smells. Nothing out of place. No interlopers here.

Longarm started to dig a cheroot out of his coat pocket as he dropped his gaze to the trail off the stage's right front wheel. He frowned, leaving the cigar in his pocket.

Mitchum was walking the team through a flat stretch preceding the next steep grade, so Longarm had time to scrutinize the three shod hoof prints deeply etched in the mud beside the trail, angling from the slope to the right of it and toward the stage road itself. Longarm craned his neck to see behind, as the stage kept moving at its slow, plodding pace, and saw more prints delineating the rider's route across the trail, through a trickling rivulet, and up a needle-covered slope into deep, dark forest.

Judging by the depth of the tracks, and the lack of water in them, the rider had come down the northern slope, crossed the trail, and ridden up the southern slope earlier that morning. Not much earlier. Maybe only an hour or so ago.

Longarm turned his head forward, chewing his mustache. Could have been anyone, of course. The West was full of drifters. Still, this was remote country. Not many ranches through here. Those dark, muddy tracks gave Longarm a sour feeling. They made the hair along the back of his neck bristle.

"What's the matter, Custis?" Mitchum asked him.

"Nothin'."

"Nothin', hell!"

Longarm glanced behind him once more at the dark balsams and spruces pushing up close to the trail. A good place to set up a bushwhack, those woods. Was his friend, Bella's cowardly killer, about to take another shot from that southern slope?

He turned his head forward again, perusing the slope on the trail's left side.

"Shut up and drive, Hank."

"Yessir, badly washed and rutted," Mitchum said later, when he'd pulled the stage up to a fork in the trail. "Look at them blowdowns, them boulders." The gray-bearded jehu shook his head darkly. "No, sir. We won't be headin' up to Hell Creek today."

Longarm stared past the worn wooden sign pointing toward the trail rising up the southern slope and announcing HELL CREEK 5 MI. Several fir and spruce trees had blown down from the slopes on either side of the trail, blocking it. Clay-colored boulders, too, had rolled down the slopes, further making the trace impassable. At least for the stage. A creek ran down alongside the trail, flooding it in places.

"Sorry, Miss Hunter," Mitchum hollered down to the coach. "Trail's impassable. We'll have to continue on to Bob's Gulch Station, I'm afraid. Maybe you can find a way to Hell Creek from there!"

"But, Mr. Mitchum, I must reach Hell Creek today," came the girl's anguished reply from below. "I have nowhere else to go!"

"Sorry, miss. You couldn't get a farm wagon up that slope today!"

Mitchum was about to whip the reins against the team's backs, when Longarm grabbed his arm. "Hold on, Hank."

"What is it?"

"I have a spare horse." Longarm stood and set his rifle on his shoulder. "Might as well use it to escort the girl up to her destination."

"What the hell—federal deputies playin' chaperone these days?" the driver said as Longarm climbed down the side of the stage.

"Why the hell not?"

"I ain't gonna be responsible for that mail train loot, damnit, Custis!"

"No, you ain't." Longarm opened the carriage door. Sarah Hunter sat frowning at him pensively, skeptically. "Come on out, Miss Hunter. If you wanna get on up to Hell Creek so crazy bad, I might as well escort you, since I have the extra horse an' all."

Since it looked as though she was going to sit there beside the old woman, suspiciously pondering the lawman's offer for a time, Longarm left the door open and walked back to untie both horses from the metal rings on the outside of the luggage boot. He walked the horses away from the stage and dead-reined them, then hauled his and Bella's saddles out of the boot. He also removed the saddlebags containing the mail train loot. It was his duty to see that the money was returned to its rightful owners, and he'd do that just as soon as he saw the girl to safety.

Or had run down the mysterious bushwhacker.

Whichever came last . . .

When he saw the old man step out of the stage then turn to help Miss Hunter down, Longarm pulled her carpetbag and steamer trunk out of the boot, as well. The old man climbed back aboard and closed the door behind him.

"This what you wanna do, miss?" Mitchum called from the driver's box.

"Yes," she said, still studying Longarm dubiously. "Yes, I suppose it is. I guess I really have no other choice, if I wish to reach Hell Creek."

"Gonna be a light load I pull in to the end of the line,

I reckon," Mitchum said. "So long, Custis! Farewell, Miss Hunter!"

Mitchum stood and yelled and shook the reins over the team's backs, and the coach rocked and rattled and rolled on down the trail. Because the stage road was still soggy, there wasn't any dust to speak of.

Miss Hunter walked up to where Longarm was throwing the saddle on Bella's dappled black. "I don't understand, Longarm. Why are you doing this? Surely, you must have more important things to do than escort me to Hell Creek."

"Not at the moment," Longarm said, not wanting to admit to the girl that, in a way, he was using her as bait to lure in the drygulcher. If she was the killer's target, that was. If it was Longarm himself and/or the loot, well, then, he supposed he was putting her in harm's way.

It was a risk he'd have to take, because something told him there was a relatively good chance the girl's life was in danger anyway, though beyond a strange tightening behind his belly button and a prickling of the hairs under his shirt collar, he had no hard reason to think so.

When Longarm had finished saddling the girl's black and had attached Bella's bedroll and saddlebags behind the cantle, he tossed his own saddle blanket and McClellan saddle atop the bay. He noticed the girl staring at him from beside her steamer trunk, her green eyes anxious.

"While I am obliged to you," she said, her voice quavering a little, "I must ask you—you are a gentleman, aren't you, Longarm? I mean . . . as a matter of form, I . . . uh . . . really shouldn't be doing this."

"Doing what?"

"Why, traveling without chaperone with a man, of course. I mean, back where I come from, it might be looked upon with derision. In fact, my morals might even be called into question, as well as your own."

She let a hand travel up absently and touch the two top buttons of her short traveling jacket, as though to make sure she wasn't showing him anything she shouldn't be. Like the two beautiful orbs he'd seen last night, he thought with a pang of chagrin.

"Now, Miss Hunter," Longarm said, as he slid his Winchester down snug in his saddle sheath, "do you see anyone out here who might be offended by us traveling together?"

She glanced around as though to be sure there was no one spying on them from the forest. "Um . . . well, no . . ."

"There you have it." Longarm glanced at the trunk sitting in the trail beside her. "Now, that there might be a little hard to haul on horseback to Hell Creek."

She looked down at the item in question.

"One possibility," the lawman said, "is you could ride double with me, and I could strap the trunk aboard the black. Otherwise, we'll have to leave it, I'm afraid."

"Oh, I couldn't leave it! There isn't much in it—just a few things I managed to salvage from the cyclone. My clothes, of course. A few books. But mostly cherished family items—Momma's Bible and hair brush, and Pa's watch, and . . ."

"All right, then."

Fifteen minutes later, they were headed up the trail.

The girl rode behind Longarm on the bay, straddling his bedroll and saddlebags. She held the reins of the black that trailed behind, the steamer trunk strapped and roped atop Bella's saddle.

As they traversed flat ground, her free hand clutched Longarm's saddle, occasionally gripping his brown tweed coat. But when they climbed a steep hill, which they often did, as Hell Creek lay a good thousand feet higher than the main stage road, she had to wrap her arm around his waist and lean in close against his back. The feel of her arm against his belly and her breasts pushing against his back, coupled with the remembered image of the lovely breasts naked from the night before, made the lawman's pants grow tight.

He kept his eyes on the terrain around him, however—forever on the lookout for the mysterious bushwhacker with the large-caliber rifle.

Chapter 12

Longarm figured they probably could have reached Hell Creek by dark if they'd kept riding up the rising and falling, twisting and turning wagon road. But around three o'clock another storm rolled in. Massive purple clouds slid across the cobalt sky, turning the light from golden to charcoal. Thunder grumbled and boomed, echoing around the steep, piney ridges. As the first rain-drops began to slash at Longarm and his blond charge, the lawman headed for a cave he'd spied along the side of the deep gorge they'd been traversing.

It was a well-sheltered cavern gouged out of a gran-ite scarp, with a waterfall nearby tumbling over an eroded stone ridge and dropping thirty feet into a sandy pool, before running off into a fast-falling, rocky creek that twisted among dense spruces and tamaracks. A couple of pines standing near the scarp offered a mod-icum of shelter for the horses. As soon as Longarm had tied and unsaddled the mounts, he hauled his and the girl's gear into the cave. She was already building a fire from wood that someone had stacked inside, near a charred stone fire ring.

Obviously, the cave had been used before. It was the custom of the country to leave such shelters stocked with dry wood. Longarm hoped he could return the favor. Sometimes travelers even left food in such places. But there was no food here, so while the girl tended the fire, he headed out to see if he could haul in a rabbit before the storm really got hammering.

He hunted the forest near the cave for fifteen minutes before the rain started to pour. He'd just swung around to head back to the cave, when he spied a wild turkey running out from beneath a spruce toward a currant snag, taking long strides with its neck extended.

Longarm whipped up his rifle, took hasty aim, leading his quarry by a hair, and fired.

The turkey squawked and dropped dead.

Back in the cave, he plucked and cut up the bird, and fried it in his tin skillet with the bird's own fat. He had nothing to cook along with it, but Sarah didn't seem to mind. She was obviously accustomed to making do, likely having endured tough years on her family's farm in Minnesota. She ate her half of the fried bird hungrily, casting aside proper table manners and using her hands. She even sat with her legs crossed beneath her dress, her hair hanging somewhat wildly about her pretty face with green eyes sparkling in the firelight.

In the darkening cave with the storm blasting outside, eating with her fingers and taking deep slurps of her black coffee, Longarm thought she looked every bit the stalwart farm girl, unafraid of getting a little grease on her fingers or shit between her toes. Good thing, too. She would need every grain of sand she had to build a life for herself in Hell Creek.

He studied her curiously as he ate, the fire caressing her pale, even features, flashing in her long, expressive eyes. What could possibly have possessed her to come out here? Tragedy usually turned people toward others, not away from them. It didn't usually make them want to become even more isolated and alone.

Even if they were sent the deed to a cattle ranch.

He remembered what she'd said on the Ten Horses' front gallery the afternoon before about not marrying "some worthless cad." The fervor with which she'd made the pronouncement told him her relations with the opposite sex might have been less than satisfactory. Likely, she'd had her heart broken. It took girls her age some time to mend. Maybe, once she saw Hell Creek and the ranch that was now hers, her heart would mend itself right quickly, and she'd head back to where she'd come from.

Longarm decided to just go ahead and ask. What could it hurt? The most she could do was tell him to go to hell. "Who was he?"

She looked at him over the small drumstick in her hands. Her ripe mouth was touchingly grease-stained, and she didn't seem to care. She wrinkled the skin above the bridge of her nose. "Whoever are you talking about?"

"The worthless cad you mentioned last night."

She compressed her mouth, turned its corners down.

"William Montgomery Murray, if you must know." With her teeth, she ripped off more meat from the drumstick. Chewing, she said, "He was an older boy who lived just up the creek from my family's farm. He asked for my hand. I'd told everyone. Planned a church wedding. Ma had even sewn me a beautiful dress of cream taffeta with a long velvet train and a lace veil."

She chewed, staring at the nearly denuded drumstick in her fingers. "Two days before the wedding I found him down by the creek behind his farm with the hired German girl who cleaned house for his mother. I'd heard her screaming and thought the Sioux had attacked." She shook her head, a look of disgust on her face as she continued to pluck the remaining strips of meat from the bone with her teeth. "Nope. My dear William simply had her bent forward over a tree stump, her house dressed shoved up around her waist, his own pants on the ground around his boots."

She gave a fateful sigh. "And here I thought he'd been savin' himself for our wedding night, as I had been."

"I am sorry, Sarah."

She dropped the cleaned drumstick on her plate and wiped her hands on a chunk of split pine lying beside the snapping fire. "The way I see it, I'm just damn lucky I found out what kind of a man he was *before* I went and married the copper-riveted fool instead of *after*."

Longarm set his own plate aside, then used a leather swatch to lift the coffeepot from the fire and refill her cup. "You're right about him bein' a fool, Sarah. I can't imagine a bigger fool anywhere on earth to cheat on a girl such as you." He gave her a tender, sympathetic wink.

She stared at him through the steam rising from her cup, color rising in her cheeks. "Thanks, Longarm."

"I mean it." He stood and grabbed his rifle, then turned to the cave opening. It had nearly stopped raining, and thunder rumbled only distantly, the storm having passed. The thinning clouds showed some wan green light in the sky above the canyon, but it would be gone soon, as the sun was down. "I'm gonna head out and check on the horses," he said.

"All right. I'll clean the plates off in the waterfall."

"Don't go far."

She frowned at him with faint suspicion. "Any particular reason I shouldn't, Longarm?"

Longarm hiked his shoulder nonchalantly. "Just gettin' dark, that's all. Easy to get lost."

He headed on out of the cave, and while the girl washed their plates under the waterfall that had grown louder after the rain, Longarm gave the horses a quick inspection then tramped on away from the cave. He held his rifle in both hands across his chest as he followed a game path down along the narrow stream that fairly roared with fresh runoff.

There was just enough light left that he could make out tan patches of ground between the darker trees and boulders. There was no breeze at all, and when he had drifted a ways from the stream, he could hear the dull thud of a distant pinecone tumbling from a branch far up the near-black, forested southern ridge.

He looked along the trail that he and the girl had been following and was glad to see only the tracks of his bay and the girl's black. No rider had come up the trail behind them or, judging by the sign, was anywhere around the cave.

Longarm sat on a boulder with his back to a scarp, fished a half-smoked cheroot from the breast pocket of his coat, lit up, and smoked as he sat listening and watching the night growing blacker, feeling the high-country air becoming cooler. He heard little but the soft thumping and crunching of what he judged to be deer or elk moving up the far ridge through the forest, and the crunching, tumbling sound of a sodden, rotten branch falling from a distant tree.

When he returned to the cave, Sarah was curled up in Bella's bedroll, her back to the fire that had burned down to glowing coals. Her dress lay folded neatly beside the saddle she used as a pillow. One bare leg poked out from the bottom of her wool blankets. Her blond hair was fanned out across the saddle as her shoulders rose and fell slowly, regularly, as she slept.

Longarm quietly added more wood to the fire, as the night would get cold, then shucked out of his clothes, still damp from the wet ride earlier. He laid out everything, including his long underwear, around the fire, then rolled up naked in his soogan, resting his head back against his saddle. His rifle leaned against the cave wall nearby, and his shell belt and six-gun were coiled on the ground beside him. He wore only his hat, which he tipped down over his eyes.

Sleep, like a warm, soft hand, stole over him.

He woke later, blinking up at the cave's low ceiling, across which the dying fire shunted dim, amber light and heavy shadows. A half second later, he straightened, grabbed his Winchester, and lowered the cocking lever—but froze before he could slam it back against the underside of the rifle.

He realized that it wasn't the sound of an intruder that had awakened him. It was the girl moaning on the other side of the nearly dead fire. Quietly, he depressed the Winchester's hammer and leaned the rifle back against the side of the cave. He stared at her on the other side of the fire, and a hot wave of desire swept over him.

Sarah lay on her back, only half-covered by her blankets. She'd slid down so that her head lay not on the saddle but on the bare ground. A pair of frilly white undergarments lay in a rumpled pile beside her as though they'd been cast hurriedly aside. Her eyes were closed, but her face was a mask of what first appeared severe anguish, until he saw that her legs were spread wide, knees raised. The blanket concealed her crotch but not her belly, which rose and fell sharply as she breathed as though she were running a great distance and clawed at herself with both hands.

She grunted and sighed and made little, desperate moaning sounds as she manipulated herself, half-asleep but not in agony at all. Her knees bobbed as she clawed at herself. Nearly her entire right leg was exposed, and she was curling her little toes so hard they were white.

Ecstasy.

Longarm looked down at his own crotch. His cock was fully erect and bobbing as the blood surged in it. Before he knew what he was doing, he'd crawled over to her, drawn her blanket back away from her, and lain down beside her. He turned toward her, his erect member pushing against her.

She gasped and opened her eyes. She gasped again when she saw him staring down at her, felt his cock against her hip.

He slid her hair away from her right cheek with the back of his hand. "You shouldn't have to do that, Sarah. No girl as pretty as you should ever have to do that."

She blinked. The fire's reflection painted her pupils amber. "I was dreaming of you, Longarm."

"You don't have to dream no longer, Sarah."

"Oh, God." Suddenly, her eyes grew fearful. "I've never done it before!"

"Shhh." Longarm sandwiched her face in his hands, leaned down, and kissed her tender, moist lips. "I'll go slow, show you how. It ain't gonna hurt a bit."

"Oh, God," she whispered. "I'm afraid."

"Nothin' to be afraid of."

She reached over and closed her hand on his cock. Her eyes widened in shock. She lowered her chin and looked down at him, her lips parted as she breathed. "It's so . . . big."

"Like I said, I'll go slow."

Propped on one elbow, he reached down her belly with his other hand and slid his fingers over her silky snatch. He slipped his index finger inside her, felt the soft, hot wetness. She sucked a sharp breath, and her bare breasts rose as she opened her mouth and flicked her passionate eyes at the ceiling.

"Oh," she said, as he stroked her very slowly—up and down and in and out, running his finger over the soft, pliant lobes of her flesh. "Oh . . . oh . . ." She bit down on a knuckle and stared down in wide-eyed fascination at his big, brown hand. "Oh . . . *God* . . . !"

She had his cock in her left hand, and she squeezed it while he fingered her. His own blood boiled in his veins. He saw the flush rise in her cheeks as he worked her. When his hand was wet enough that he knew she was ready for him, he rolled on top of her and propped himself up on his arms and knees.

"You ready, Sarah?" he whispered, kissing her softly then nuzzling her neck, brushing her soft skin with his handlebar mustache and nibbling her earlobe. "It ain't too late to back out, you know."

"Oh, God, no!" she said, grabbing him again and staring up at him desperately. "Please, Longarm!"

"All right."

He lifted her legs with his hands, sliding them up his arms and over his shoulders. She stared at him, half-frightened, half-ecstatic, flicking her eyes down to his throbbing, jutting shaft. He slid forward until her knees were hooked over his shoulders, and then he slid his cock snug against her snatch until its swollen head parted the tender flesh and very slowly disappeared inside her.

Her mouth opened wide and she lifted her chin, arching her back. The sinews stood out in her neck. A forked vein swelled in her forehead. But she said nothing.

He continued to slide inside her, watching her large,

red-tipped breasts rise and fall sharply as she breathed, feeling her clenching and unclenching the muscles in her long legs. When he'd gone as far as he could go, he slid out of her completely. Her body convulsed as she looked up at him in desperation, her green eyes wide with beseeching as they flicked between his own eyes and his cock, its tip just touching her soaked pubic hair.

He smiled and slid his cock back into her, and she lifted her chin again and groaned so loudly that the sound echoed several times around the cave.

She lay nearly inert at first, tentative, a little afraid. But as he continued to make love to her, she found her own rhythm and sort of bucked her pelvis against him. When they'd been going at it for about five minutes, slowly, him giving her time to get used to the act in general and to him in particular, she swallowed and stared up at him, and surprised him with: "Were you watching me last night, Longarm?"

"Yes," he said, grunting as he thrust himself into her once more. It didn't even occur to him to lie to her.

She smiled in delight and squeezed her breasts in her hands, moaning and groaning louder and louder until he brought her to shuddering, screaming climax, his own jism pumping into her.

"You've done that before, Longarm," she said with a sigh, gently pulling at his thick, dark hair with her hands and groaning.

"Once or twice."

Later, he retrieved his rifle and leaned it against the cave wall near where he lay down again with Sarah. She laid her head on his chest, and he wrapped an arm around her, holding her close. Exhausted, they fell fast asleep.

He woke again later and lifted his head, blinking his eyes. The storm had apparently returned. Sharp, blue lightning flashed over the canyon, for a brief instant silhouetting a man's hatted figure crouched over a rifle in the cave's opening.

Chapter 13

Longarm grabbed the Winchester from against the wall.

He was expecting the man standing in the cave entrance to shoot the rifle that he himself was wielding, but as the lawman levered a round into the breech, he vaguely thought that he might have gotten a better look at the intruder than the intruder had gotten of him in the dark cave.

The cook fire had gone out entirely, not even leaving any glowing coals.

Longarm wasted no time, not bothering to call out. He fired the Winchester three times quickly, shooting and levering, the rifle's screeching blasts thundering off the near walls like dynamite explosions. The first of his own gun flashes had shown him the man still standing crouched in the cave's mouth, the storm resuming behind him. His second flash showed the man jolting straight backward. The third flash showed Longarm nothing at all but the dark cave entrance and the gray rain slashing down at an angle.

When the rifle's blasts stopped echoing, they were replaced by Sarah's screams. Longarm looked to his right to see her vague, dark figure cowering in the wool blankets, her head in her arms. He had no time to console her, but leaped to his feet and ran naked to the cave entrance, and looked out.

There down the steep, gravelly grade leading toward the stream lay the sprawled figure of the interloper. A couple of broad lightning flashes revealed a rangy man in a yellow rain slicker lying on his back, one denim-clad leg straight, the other bent outward at the knee. He wasn't moving.

Quickly, Longarm moved back into the cave and began fumbling around for his underwear. His eyes had adjusted to the darkness so that he could see some definition to the shadows around him.

"What is it?" Sarah cried, sitting up and whipping her head around in the darkness. "What's happening?"

"Not sure yet, but you're safe . . . for now. Build up the fire, will ya, girl?"

Longarm pulled on his socks, boots, hat, and rain slicker, then walked out of the cave and down the slope to crouch over the man lying there. He wore black boots with silver spurs. A green bandanna was knotted around his neck. His broad-brimmed tan Stetson had fallen off and lay beside him. The front of his slicker was streaked with blood diluted by the rain.

Farther down the grade, near the stream, lay what

appeared to be a Spencer .56 carbine. A caliber large enough to punch a fist-sized hole through a man's brisket. Or a girl's, for that matter.

Longarm opened the first three buttons of the slicker and looked between the garment's flaps to see a red-and-black checked shirt.

Longarm's pulse throbbed in his temples.

He was staring down at the bushwhacker.

He lifted the man by his collar and shook him, trying to revive him. "Who the hell are you, damnit?" Longarm yelled in frustration above the storm. "Who're you after?"

Nothing. The man's head merely wobbled. His silver-gray soup-strainer mustache and the Burnside whiskers framing his long, horsey face were sodden. Longarm dropped him, heard his head thud against the soaked sand and gravel.

Longarm opened the man's coat and emptied his pockets but came up with nothing more to identify him but a single stub of pencil, a small notebook, a wad of bills, a small hide sack of silver coins, and a playing card—the ace of hearts. He stuffed the possibles into a pocket of his raincoat then strode back up the hill and into the cave, at the outside edge of which the girl stood, holding a blanket around her hunched shoulders. Her legs and feet were bare.

"Is he dead?" she asked, eyes bright with terror. She was shivering, no doubt from fear as well as from the chill of the wet night.

She'd built a small fire of pine twigs, and the flames

snapped and sputtered, issuing thin tendrils of white smoke.

"He's a goner. Come on over here by the fire and get warm, Sarah. I'll make a pot of coffee."

She stood staring out at the rain. "What if there's more . . . like him . . . out there?"

"If there is, you'd be a hell of a lot safer in here by the fire than out there in the open."

She gasped and scampered over to the fire, and sat down near where Longarm was pouring water from his canteen into the coffeepot. She sat with her knees raised, ankles crossed, holding the blanket around her shoulders, nearly covering her breasts. Between her legs Longarm could see the firelight glinting on her little, furred, pink snatch, but he kept his mind on his coffee and the dead man.

Longarm had seen only the one bushwhacker and one set of tracks before, so he figured the man to be a loner. If he hadn't been alone, anyone riding with him would have no doubt made his presence known by now.

"Who was he, Longarm? What was he doing out on such a cold, wet night?"

"Can't say as I know for sure, but I aim to find out," the lawman said, setting the pot on the fire to boil.

He'd told the girl the truth. All he knew was that the dead man was the same killer who'd shot Bella. He still didn't know what the man had been after, tracking Longarm and Sarah to the cave.

"Maybe he was only looking for shelter," Sarah offered. "Are you sure he needed *killing*?"

"I'm sure."

"What if he was just looking to get *warm*?"

"Trust me. He wasn't just looking to get warm."

"How do you *know*?"

Longarm looked at her staring at him wild-eyed across the fire. "Because he's the same hombre who shot Bella."

Her lower jaw dropped slightly as she pondered the information. As the coffeepot started to steam and gurgle, Longarm pulled the dead man's possibles out of the pocket of his rain slicker. He spilled the wad of bills and pouch of coins, the pencil and the small notepad and the ace of hearts onto his bedroll.

The card likely meant nothing. He'd known more than one hombre of a superstitious nature to carry a playing card around for luck—maybe the same card they'd used to fill in a royal flush with at one time.

Flipping through the bills, Longarm counted fifty-seven dollars. No small pile. There was another eleven-fifty in coin. The man was obviously not just some grubline-riding drifter. With that much cash, he could be holed up in a warm, dry hotel in Salt Lake or Cheyenne.

Longarm picked up the notepad, a good half of the sheets of which had been torn out. The very first page had a map scribbled on it in pencil. Crude as the drawing was, Longarm recognized several of the formations indicated. They lay between a circled X labeled "Casper" penciled on the upper left hand corner of the page, and another circled X labeled "Hell Creek" down on the bottom right corner of the page.

"What is it?" Sarah asked.

Longarm studied the map for a time then flipped the

wrinkled cardboard cover closed on the pad and stuck it back in his pocket. He looked across the fire at the girl, trying to figure out a way to ask the question on his mind without sending her into a panic.

Sarah, you don't know why anyone would hire a killer to turn you toe-down, do you?

"What is it, Longarm?" she urged. "What're you thinking?"

"Nothin'," he said. "I was just . . . uh . . . tryin' to get a handle on the dead man—that's all. Nothin' more than that."

"I know what you're thinking."

He looked at her again. "You do?"

She nodded. "You're thinking he was after that loot you have in the saddlebags. It's obvious, isn't it?" She slid her own troubled eyes to the saddlebags in question leaning against the wall near Longarm and his Winchester. "He must've seen you with them somewhere, and he's been stalking you, looking for an opportunity to make off with all that money. A highwaymen. A common outlaw. I've read all about them in the *Police Gazette*!"

Longarm smiled weakly. "Took the words right out of my mouth."

"Well, you got him before he could get you." She sat up straighter, her eyes suddenly bold and encouraging. "Because that's the kind of lawman you are. You left him, as the magazine writers say, 'smokin' in hell.'"

"I reckon that's where he is, all right."

"Awful as it is, he's dead." Sarah let the blanket fall from her shoulders. She grinned across the fire at him lustily, her breasts bare, her pink snatch gaping at him from between her spread thighs. "I reckon we might as well do it again, don't you think? Might help us get back to sleep after all the commotion?"

She stood and walked around the fire to him and stood over him—naked and peach-skinned and perfect, breasts jutting. Her blond crotch was level with his eyes. Behind her, lightning flashed, and thundered rumbled, and the rain streamed down.

His cock was stirring like a snake in its hole.

How could he resist her?

He shucked out of his rain slicker, socks, boots, and balbriggans while she stood over him, smiling down at him, her feet slightly spread. When he was naked, he shoved his head up against her crotch and, placing his hands firmly against her cool buttocks, held her before him while he worked his tongue ever so slowly into her.

She groaned and ran her hands through his hair.

After he'd licked her into a frenzy, he lay her down on his blankets, spread her legs with his own, and fucked her to the beat of the storm's wild symphony.

Chapter 14

The next morning, while Sarah finished her second cup of coffee and the rabbit she'd warmed up for them both for breakfast, Longarm went out and dragged the dead bushwhacker off.

He left the man with most of his gear, including the Spencer .56, but he relieved him of the silver-chased Peacemaker that he wore in a holster thonged low on his right thigh. Longarm was not one to weigh himself down with weaponry, but the sweet-looking Peacemaker was too much gun for the mountain lions. He had no intention of wearing such a garish weapon, but he'd stow it in his saddlebags until he found someone to give it to.

He'd consider presenting it to the somewhat prissy young man who played the typewriter in Billy Vail's outer office. Maybe such a weapon was just what Henry needed to put some spring in his step, though Longarm would certainly have to teach him how to shoot it first.

When he'd disposed of the mysterious regulator—
what else could the dead man be but a hired killer?—
Longarm gathered some deadfall branches, wet as they
were, and stacked them loosely beside the fire ring inside the cave. Likely, they'd dry here in the cave before
they were needed by others seeking shelter from the
mountain monsoons.

He found the killer's grulla, a rangy, clean-lined
horse, tied a ways down canyon. There was nothing in
the man's saddle gear, including his saddlebags, to give
any better indication of who he was or what he did for
a living. Longarm settled the mount down—he was
pitchy from the storm as well as the strange man fooling with him—and led him back to the cave.

Ten minutes later, he and the girl rode back out of
the still-dripping pines, to the main trail. He had the
girl ride the grulla and he'd lashed her trunk to the late
Bella's black. As they climbed up out of the canyon,
they rode into the golden morning sunshine that shone
like liquid gold on the wet conifers.

They paused to watch a herd of twenty or thirty elk
cropping the lush grass of a broad mountain park com-
plete with a shallow creek shimmering along its eastern
fringe. Bella had never seen an elk before, and she stared
in open amazement at the majestic creatures.

"You know what, Longarm?" she said softly after
they watched the foraging beasts for five minutes or so.
"I think I'm going to like it up here."

"I hope you do, Sarah."

He didn't add that there were other things to consider
beyond the flora and fauna. There was no point in tell-

ing her that he suspected that the man he'd killed the
night before had been out to kill her, likely for pay—
until he was sure. The killer hadn't accomplished his
task, but that didn't mean that whoever wanted her dead
wouldn't hire someone else.

As they continued riding up the trail toward Hell
Creek, he wondered what kind of reception they'd receive.

They followed the trail through another sun-bathed park
two hours later and into some lodgepole pines and firs,
before emerging from the fragrant forest and into the
outskirts of Hell Creek. Longarm had smelled the aroma
of cook fires a while back, and now he saw the smoke
issuing from several of the shake-roofed buildings
spread out before him, on either side of the trail that, a
few yards farther on, became Hell Creek's main drag.
The creek itself twisted through wolf willows and rabbitbrush along the town's left edge, along a jog of low,
pine-covered hills, and the remains of several place
mines, including Long Toms and "rocker" boxes, moldered out there in the brush.

Hell Creek had been a sizeable boomtown only a few
years before. Most of the original buildings remained,
but Longarm was swept by an eerie feeling as he stared
down the broad trail at the twenty or thirty dwellings
and false-fronted businesses that appeared weathered
and dilapidated and, for the most part, abandoned.

There wasn't a soul on the street for the entire length
of the town. Just now a small dog of indeterminate
breeding crossed at an angle from a small shack with a
barber pole on the right to what Longarm remembered

as a hardware store on the left, though now its door was shut, its windows boarded up, weeds growing through the rotting planks of the front stoop.

The last and only time he'd been here, he'd had a devil of a time getting through town for the glut of ore drays and bearded miners milling in the streets, with brightly, skimpily clad whores yelling enticements from a half dozen balconies on either side of the street.

There'd been a potpourri of smells—cook fires, perfume, stale beer, axle grease, horses, and privies. Now there was only the smell of the cook fires, and they were faint smells, at that.

He and Sarah had stopped their horses at the edge of the woods to inspect the town. Now he glanced at the girl sitting the grulla that was switching its tail at the blackflies.

"Well, what do you think, Sarah?"

When she turned toward him, he thought she looked a little stricken. But she smiled. "It looks very peaceful and quiet. Just what I need!"

Longarm glanced back at the saddlebags riding behind him, and bulging with the mail train loot. His first order of business here in Hell Creek would be to secure the stolen money. Then . . . he hoped like hell there was a cook in town, because his spine was beginning to get all too friendly with his belly. Remembering that the jailhouse sat on a side street about halfway through town, he clucked the bay forward.

"Come on, girl. Before we get you settled out at your ranch, I'm gonna see if this bustling little burg still has a lawman."

"Yes," Sarah said with forced brightness. "Let's take a little tour."

As they rode on through the heart of the town, Longarm was glad to see both a working general store and a little café with smoke twisting from its rusty tin chimney pipe. At least the girl would have a place to buy supplies, and, more immediately, neither he nor she would starve.

There was even a livery barn, he noted. It lay farther on along the street, beyond where he swung left down a side street and saw a little, stone building with a narrow wooden porch. The hovel lay near where Hell Creek curved through town from the east, the side street crossing it with the help of a gray wooden bridge consisting merely of heavy planks. A shingle jutting from the building's porch roof into the muddy street and supported by a pealed pine pole announced HELL CREEK TOWN MARSHAL.

The sign looked a little gray-weathered and faded, but not as much as most of the other signs staring down at him and Sarah or jutting toward them from boarded up facades. Some were missing their support posts and dangled toward the ground at a steep angle. Someone, probably back in Hell Creek's heyday, had shot a hole through the "s" in MARSHAL.

The jailhouse door stood open—another good indication that the town still had a population, however small. An even better indication was that a man stepped out the open door and sauntered onto the hovel's rotting porch. He was a short, slender, but tough-looking man dressed in black pants and a black leather vest over a

white shirt. A five-pointed star that appeared to have
been cut out of an airtight tin was pinned to his vest.

He wore a black, funnel-brimmed Stetson atop a
small haystack of blond curls. Giant mustaches of the
same color hung down over the sides of his mouth, and
an eight-inch spade beard adorned his chin.

The local lawman walked over to the top of the
porch's three steps, one of the steps missing one of its
two planks, and stopped. Poking his hat brim up off his
freckled forehead, he leaned against a roof support post,
folded his arms on his chest, and grinned up at the newcomers.

"Well, I'll be goddamned," Longarm said, poking
his own hat brim up to get a better look at the man.
"Jared Wilborn?"

The man chuckled, squinting his devilishly slanted,
dark blue eyes that looked all the bluer set against that
darkly freckled, sun-seasoned skin. "Custis P. Fucking
Long . . . uh, please do forgive my French, miss"—he
pinched his hat brim to Sarah—"it's been a long damn
time."

"It sure has. And I'd sooner have expected Jesus H.
Christ himself . . . uh, please do forgive our talk, Miss
Sarah . . . to be wearing the badge of Hell Creek, than
you, you old outlaw!"

Wilborn gave Longarm a friendly but pointed look.
"Now, you know I ain't ridden the long coulees for a
long damn time, Custis."

"Sure, sure. In fact, last I saw you, you were a stock
inspector over Nevada way."

Longarm quickly reflected on the time he and Wilborn had ridden together, six or seven years ago, chasing down rustlers in the desert country southwest of Provo. But Wilborn knew as well as Longarm did that the man had been an owlhoot before that—and a killer of some repute. Longarm hadn't known him then, but in Utah he'd sensed he couldn't trust the man as far as he could throw him uphill against a Texas twister.

"How'd you end up here . . . ?" Longarm said, shuttling his gaze around the all-but-deserted buildings. "In this back of beyond sorta place?"

"Just rode through about a year ago. Apparently the previous badge-toter had just died howlin' like a dog from the syph." Wilborn hiked a narrow shoulder and hooked his hand over the Colt Navy he wore for the cross draw high on his left hip. He wore another hogleg, a horn-handled Russian .44, thonged low on his right thigh. "The town council asked me if I wanted the job, and since here's as good as anywhere to sink a root, I said why the hell not?"

He squinted as he followed Longarm's glance around the town. "Nice, quiet place. Even quieter since most of the gold pinched out and there was a big strike farther down the mountain."

He looked at Longarm and grinned with one side of his mouth, showing several large, yellow teeth. "I ain't as young as I once was, you know, Custis. Sometimes a man just wants a quiet place to sit fer a spell." He jerked a thumb at the wicker rocking chair on the porch to his right. "You might want to start thinkin' about that yourself. Say, that's a mighty purty partner you're ridin' with."

He glanced with his whole mouth as his large, lusty,

dark blue eyes settled on Sarah. "I don't believe we've been introduced proper."

"Sarah, meet the chief law enforcement officer of your new hometown," Longarm said, seeing no reason to keep the girl's identity secret. Wilborn and the other townsfolk would learn soon enough who she was. "Marshal Wilborn, meet your newest citizen—Sarah Hunter."

Longarm stared at Wilborn, noting a subtle change in the man's expression at the mention of Sarah's last name. At least, Longarm thought it was a change—a very slight flush and a slight narrowing of the man's eyes as he relieved the support post of his weight, standing up straight and as tall as he could at five-seven or so.

Or was Longarm only imagining a change in the man's demeanor?

Wilborn moved down the steps and lifted a hand to Sarah, who extended her own with a warm smile. "Pleased to make your acquaintance, Miss Hunter. All the citizens of Hell Creek, few as they are, call me Jared. I hope you do the same."

"Jared it is," Sarah said.

"I ain't quite sure I understand," Wilborn said, glancing back along the sidestreet behind Longarm and the girl, as though expecting to see more newcomers than just these two before him. "Did I hear correctly—you're moving to Hell Creek. *Permanent-like?*"

"Oh, not to Hell Creek proper, Marshal. I'm moving out to my uncle, Lester Debo's, ranch. He willed it to me before his passing last spring."

"Debo?"

"Yes, Lester Debo. I have the deed to his ranch right

here," Sarah said, reaching into the carpetbag hanging from her saddlehorn and pulling out a folded, legal-sized sheet of paper. "From what I can make out of all these directions and figures, it's a twenty-acre parcel south of town, along the North Fork of Hell Creek."

"Huh," Wilborn said, fingering his scraggly goat whiskers. "Debo. No kiddin'. Well, that's a name I never heard of. No, ma'am—if there's a Lester Debo in these parts, I sure never heard of him."

Chapter 15

When Sarah saw that the local lawdog had no interest in perusing the deed, she drew it back toward her breasts, frowning down at the man over her horse's twitching ears. "Oh, I'm sure you must have heard of Uncle Lester!"

Again, Marshal Wilborn pooched his lips and shook his head. "No, ma'am. I'm sorry. Maybe he just didn't get to town too often."

"That wouldn't be like him at all. Before Uncle Lester came out West to dig for gold, he visited my family and me quite often on our farm in Minnesota. He was a big, friendly man—quite a talker. He was also a bachelor. Since the ranch is only five miles from town, I'm sure he came here quite often."

Sarah chuckled wryly, blushing, as she held her hand to the side of her mouth. "Ma told me he was given to spirituous liquids, so I'm sure he patronized the saloons here in Hell Creek more than what would be considered good and proper back home!"

Sarah laughed again, a little nervously this time. Longarm could tell that the puzzled frown that Wilborn continued to regard her with had frazzled her nerves.

"*Debo?*" the local lawman said again, incredulous. "Are you sure that's the name your old Uncle Lester went by here in Hell Creek, miss? A lot of folks, you know, have a tendency to change their names when they come west. Fresh start an' all that . . ."

"Well, that's the name his claim is in, so I'm sure it's the name he went by here." Sarah's eyes darkened as she leaned forward in her saddle, openly showing her concern. "Are you *sure* you never heard of Lester Debo, Marshal Wil . . . I mean, Jared?"

Wilborn shook his head. "Nope. That's a new one on me. But I've only been here a year, and there's still quite a few prospectors up in them mountains I haven't met yet. Most likely your uncle just never got to town, or, if he did, we just never happened to run into each other. I'm sure someone over at the Hell Creek Saloon'll know who you're talkin' about. Plenty o' fellas ride down out of the hills later in the day and cut the dust to the saloon yonder. You'll find it back on Hell Street—the main drag behind ya, there."

The marshal canted his head at Longarm. "What's your business here, Custis? You ridin' chaperone with Miss Hunter or you dustin' the trail o' some curly wolf? I can tell you right now I ain't seen no strangers in town of late."

"I'm just ridin' chaperone, Jared. I run some trail wolves to ground a ways back, and since I'm in no hurry to head back to Denver and see what ugly chore Billy figured to saddle me with next, I thought I'd just see that Sarah gets safely settled in."

Sarah glanced at the bulging saddlebags on the bay's rump. "Oh, but you were going to find a place to—"

"That's right!" Longarm said, cutting her off. "I was going to find out if you knew the tall gent with a big Spencer who belongs to this horse Sarah's riding. Miss Hunter and I had to hole up in a cave out of the weather last night, and he came callin' on us with that fifty-six, and I had to beef him. Would have hauled him to town, but I wasn't sure there was any law here."

Longarm reached back and pulled the big, silver-chased Peacemaker out of his saddlebags and held it out to the side of the bay's head. "He also carried this flashy cannon. One of the nicest pieces I've seen bearing the Colt name."

"Well, look at that. That is a nice-lookin' weapon."

"I figure anyone who'd ever seen it would remember the man who carried it."

"I reckon it's just not my day to be helpful, Custis. Miss." Wilborn pinched his hat brim again to the girl, then returned his gaze to Longarm. "Probably just a drifter lookin' to rob you and steal your horses. An old story in these parts." He glanced at Longarm's gear, and his gaze held on the federal lawman's bulging saddle-bags. "Say, what you carryin' there, Custis? Two sets of saddlebags seems a bit much, don't it?"

Longarm flicked his eyes across to the girl, who had turned to study him curiously. His look kept her quiet about the loot.

To Wilborn, Longarm said, "It's been a long pull. Figured I'd need the extra camping gear. Well, it's been nice jawin' with you, Jared. I reckon me an' Miss Sarah here'll get us some food under our belts and see if anyone in the saloon knows where we'd find Uncle Lester's ranch. We could just follow the directions on the deed, but you know how unreliable they always are. I'm not about to start counting the number of rocks and trees from town to the North Fork of Hell Creek."

Longarm and Sarah reined their horses around.

Wilborn said, "Nice seein' you again, Custis. Maybe I'll hoist a beer or two with you in the saloon later this evenin'. Welcome to Hell Creek, miss!"

"Thank you, Jared," Sarah called over her shoulder as she and Longarm rode back toward the heart of the near-dead town, Longarm jerking the black along behind him.

As they approached Hell Street, Sarah glanced over her shoulder once more, then looked at Longarm. "He seems right nice."

"Oh, he is."

"How come you didn't tell him about the loot, then? You said you wanted a safe place to stow it."

"Just 'cause he's nice," Longarm said, "don't mean I trust him."

Longarm glanced behind to see Wilborn staring after him and Sarah, one boot cocked, his head canted speculatively. Longarm grinned and waved and then swung his horse to the right and started back along Hell Creek's main drag.

He angled the bay toward the little café, whose small

sign identified it simply as EATS. Its front door was propped open with a brick, likely to let the heat from the cookstove out. There was no porch, and a deep depression had been worn into the ground fronting the door. A gnarled cedar and a few silver sage shrubs grew up from the dirt and gravel under the two sashed front windows.

"I just don't understand this, Longarm," Sarah said, as they reined up at the hitchrack fronting the café. "If Marshal Wilborn has been here for a year, he simply *must* have heard of Uncle Lester."

Longarm swung down from the bay's saddle and looped his reins over the worn rack. "Sarah, I don't believe you ever told me how your Uncle Lester died."

Sarah let Longarm help her off the grulla's back then stood frowning up at him. "I was sent a letter by an attorney from here in Hell Creek informing me that he had possession of Uncle Lester's will as well as the deed to his ranch. He said that Uncle Lester had simply taken ill and, while on his deathbed, instructed the attorney to send the deed on to me, as there was very little hope that Uncle Lester would recover."

"You don't know what he died of specifically?"

"The attorney didn't say."

"What was this attorney's name?"

Sarah glanced around thoughtfully then returned her gaze to Longarm. "Daggett. One Mr. Homer Daggett, attorney at law."

"Daggett, eh? Well, someone inside might be able to direct us to Mr. Daggett." Longarm unbuckled the bay's belly strap and slipped the bit from its teeth so it could breathe and drink freely from the stock trough that was overfilled with rainwater. "And he, in turn, should be able to clear up the mystery surrounding your uncle Lester."

"That would be very nice indeed."

Longarm gave the other two horses the same treatment as his bay. He saw that Sarah was about to walk into the café ahead of him and grabbed her arm.

She frowned up at him curiously. He gave her a reassuring smile. "Don't mean to be impolite, but it might be wise for me to go in first. You know—just in case there's any Black Barts hanging around town."

No need to tell her just yet that he thought there might be a price on her head.

She continued to frown at him, faintly suspicious, for a moment. Then she stepped back. "Of course. Thank you, Longarm."

Longarm removed his hat and ducked under the door that had been built for a much shorter man. He stepped to the left, where the open door couldn't outline him, and looked around quickly as his eyes adjusted to the dingy shadows.

There was a crude lunch counter made from a halved pine log on his left, with a couple of wooden stools fronting it. Along the wall to his right were four small, square tables adorned in ragged oilcloth. At the last table at the room's far end sat two men—one younger, with long, sandy hair, and one older and nearly bald but with a thick, pewter mustache.

A woman had just lifted two plates from the bar, near where a black range sputtered and sizzled and had turned the little eatery into a furnace, and started walking away from the bar toward the two men seated at the back of the place. "Well, well," she said in a mannishly raspy voice, sort of half-coughing, as folks do who smoke without surcease, "we got newcomers, boys. Take a good look. We don't get to see many of those."

She laughed as she set the plates down in front of her two male customers. Both men openly stared at Longarm and Sarah, the young man having to hip around in his chair because his back was facing the front. They both had dull, dumb eyes, and Longarm thought they might be related.

They looked Longarm over thoroughly, but they fairly ogled Sarah, lusty lights dancing in their eyes.

"Go ahead and set anywhere," the woman said as she moved away from the two men, wiping her callused hands on her soiled apron. Behind the apron she wore a man's workshirt and denim jeans. "I'll be right over with some coffee."

"Obliged." Deeming the two men no immediate threat, Longarm gestured toward one of the tables, and Sarah brushed past him as she headed for it.

Longarm held the girl's chair for her, as Ma Long had raised no slouch when it came to chivalry, then sat down across from her, facing the eatery's other two customers. The woman came back from the range with two smoking stone mugs in her gnarled, lumpy hands and said with that smoker's rasp, "What'll it be? The elk steak and potatoes or the elk steak and potatoes?"

She set the cups down in front of Longarm and Sarah and winked and grinned, showing more gaps in her gums than teeth. The teeth that remained appeared ready to go the way of the others.

Longarm guessed her age, judging by the deep lines in her face and the blue pouches under her bloodshot eyes, to be somewhere around fifty. A hard fifty. She wore her red-silver hair in a ponytail down her back, with a silver clip clamping a small clump to the top of her head. The girlish fashion in which she wore her hair looked almost grotesque on a woman so wizened.

"Me, I do believe I'll have the elk steak and potatoes," Longarm said, going along with the joke. "How about you, Sarah?"

Sarah smiled up at the woman. "I believe I'll have the same."

The woman's own friendly smile faded, causing different lines in her craggy face to rearrange themselves, mostly down around the corners of her wide, thin mouth. "Sarah, huh?" she said, canting her head a little to give the blonde a thorough scrutiny. "That's a pretty name."

"Why, thank you, Miss . . ."

"Missus," the woman said. "Mrs. Kay Adams. Widow. I buried Clifton nigh on ten years ago now."

"I'm sorry to hear that, Mrs. Adams."

"No loss, really." Mrs. Adams chuckled. "Sarah, you say?"

"Sarah Hunter. I've inherited a ranch near here. Perhaps you know the man who willed it to me—Lester Debo?"

A little color rose in Kay Adams's sagging cheeks. Longarm saw her cast a quick, furtive glance at her other two customers. The bald old man stared back at her over a forkful of elk steak and potatoes. The younger man turned his head to look over his shoulder at Longarm and the girl, his eyes as cowlike as before.

"Lester Debo?" she said, manufacturing a sympathetic expression as she stared down at Sarah. "Sorry, hon, never heard of the man." She turned toward her two male customers, both still staring toward Longarm's table. "George, Billy—either of you fellas ever heard of Lester Debo?"

The men shook their heads then glanced at each other darkly before returning their attention to their plates.

"How about an attorney here in town?" Longarm asked Mrs. Adams. "Homer Daggett. Ever hear of him?"

The craggy-faced woman frowned and pooched out her lips before shaking her head. "No, sir. Never heard of no Lawyer Daggett, neither." She turned to the two men and yelled, "You two ever hear of Lawyer Daggett?"

Both men glanced at each other as they continued to shovel food into their mouths, then shook their heads.

"I reckon we're firin' on empty chambers, Sarah," Longarm said. "Are you sure it was Lawyer Daggett who sent you the deed to your uncle's ranch?"

"Yes, of course. I would never forget the name of the man who sent me such a gift."

"Sorry, folks," Mrs Adams said, throwing up her arms and then walking around the end of the makeshift bar to the range.

Chapter 16

Longarm knew that Sarah was in real trouble here in Hell Creek, by the cold, malevolent glances that both Mrs. Adams's other customers, George and Billy, gave the blonde on their way out of the eatery. Kay Adams herself was friendly enough while Longarm and Sarah ate their elk steaks and potatoes and drank their coffee, and she bid them a hearty farewell as they left.

But Longarm noted an evil undercurrent in the old woman's raspy voice—one that the girl wouldn't have noticed. And that was for the best. She'd know soon enough that she wasn't wanted here. Longarm himself was convinced enough to wonder why she wasn't.

In the meantime, he'd have to keep a close eye on her.

After he and Sarah left the café, they stabled their horses with an old half-breed who called himself Crow but didn't say much of anything else as he led Longarm's three horses up the livery barn's wooden ramp.

Crow's lone employee, who appeared also to be a half-breed and was even more taciturn than Crow himself—and who never made even passing eye contact with the two newcomers—followed Longarm and Sarah over to the Hell Creek Saloon with Sarah's steamer trunk on his shoulders. Mrs. Adams had informed Longarm and Sarah that the saloon was the only place in town that rented rooms, unless they wanted to move into one of the abandoned, rat-infested hovels lining the creek.

A shot, bull-like man with arms like tree trunks, Crow's lackey deposited the luggage in front of the saloon's bar then wheeled and shambled bull-leggedly back out the batwing doors.

"New faces in Hell Creek," said the man behind the bar. "Don't see that every day."

He was a dapper, handsome man, wide-jawed and mustachioed, in armbands and round, steel-framed glasses. Longarm placed him around thirty. His brown eyes glinted behind his glasses as he gave Sarah the hungry up-and-down.

"So we heard," Longarm said. "We'll need two rooms. One for the girl, one for me. How much?"

"Just passin' through?" the man asked, his eyes lingering on Sarah.

"I am. The girl's done movin' here for keeps. Takin' over her uncle's ranch, don't ya know."

"The ranch of Lester Debo," Sarah said hopefully. "Please don't tell me you've never heard of him."

The barman's face clouded up as he slid his gaze from the girl to Longarm then back again. "Debo?"

"You heard right," Longarm said.

"Debo, Debo, Debo," the handsome barman said, fingering one corner of his upswept mustache. "Debo, Debo, Debo . . ."

"I reckon you don't recollect meetin' up with ole Uncle Lester." Longarm had set his gear on the floor but held his sheathed rifle on his shoulder as a guidon of sorts. He was damned tired of getting run around the backyard latrine. It was time for him and Sarah to start getting some answers.

With his free hand, he pulled his leather wallet out of his coat pocket and flipped it open to reveal his badge. "Does this help refresh your memory? The name's Long. Custis P. Long. Deputy United States marshal, just like it says on that hunk of silver-chased tin."

"Ah, come on, now, Custis. Don't go gettin' all serious." The familiar voice had come from the shadows at the back of the room.

Longarm turned to see Jared Wilborn sitting at a table near the cold potbelly stove, as the Hell Creek marshal lowered a brittle, yellowed newspaper from in front of his face, grinning. "I done already asked Ned here—uh, Ned Charles, that is, the proprietor of this fine yet humble establishment—if he'd heard of Miss Sarah's Uncle Lester? Thought I'd try to save ya a little time. But he said he ain't, and you got no reason not to believe him."

"That's funny," Longarm said, his smile not reaching his eyes. "Ned here didn't sound like he'd even *heard* the name before, much less been asked about it."

Wilborn narrowed an eye. "Now, Custis, you ain't callin' me a liar, are ya?"

Longarm heard Sarah give a little, dreadful gasp. For her sake, he didn't push the Hell Creek marshal.

"Why would you lie about such a thing?" Longarm said, letting it go at that.

"There ya have it." Wilborn dropped his feet to the floor. "Is it too early for a drink, Custis? You ain't really here on official business, are ya?"

"Nah, hell. Even if I was, it's never too early for a drink. I see we got another storm rollin' in over the mountains. We'll have to wait till tomorrow to ride out and inspect Miss Sarah's new ranch, so I reckon I don't have anything to do till then *but* drink."

Longarm looked at the saloonkeeper, who was leaning forward with his pale hands on the bar. "I'll be takin' those rooms now, Ned. Sarah here would like a bath, in addition, so I'd admire for you to run a tub and some hot water up for her."

Charles slid his eyes toward Wilborn then back to Longarm. "The rooms are a dollar each. The bath is twenty-five cents extra."

Longarm tossed some gold and silver onto the unvarnished bar planks. "I reckon Uncle Sam can reimburse me later. There's for the rooms, the bath, and a bottle of your best forty-rod."

When the man had placed two keys on the bar and followed it up with a corked bottle that bore no label and that was probably 80 percent sour mash and 20 percent equal parts gunpowder and snake venom, with a few drops of skunk piss thrown in for flavor, Longarm jiggled the two keys in his palm. "Which of these has the best bed? Sarah needs to sleep well tonight so's she fresh to visit her new home tommorrow."

"Room seven probably has the best," said the barman a little indignantly.

Longarm stuck the keys in his pocket and shouldered his two sets of saddlebags. "Be back after I get Miss Sarah settled in, Jared. Go ahead and pop the cork on my bottle here."

"You need any help with them double sets o' saddlebags you got there, Custis?"

"Nah, I'll manage." Longarm didn't like the way the man was eyeing the saddlebags containing the mail train loot. He glanced at the girl's steamer trunk sitting on the floor in front of the bar. "You can haul up Miss Sarah's trunk there, though."

He smiled.

"Sure thing," Wilborn said, returning the federal's dubious grin.

The second-story hall smelled like sweat, whiskey, and coal oil. Longarm stopped at room 7, shoved one of the keys into the lock, and turned it. He pushed the door open on a room little larger than a closet. The shade was drawn over the lone window, filling the room with a depressing yellow light.

"Here ya are, Miss Sarah," Longarm said, stepping aside as the girl moved in behind him, followed by Wilborn and the trunk he held on one shoulder. "Your bath will be up shortly. I'll see to it."

As Wilborn set the trunk down with a grunt, Sarah looked up at Longarm anxiously. "What am I going to do if no one knows of Uncle Lester, Longarm?" She shook her head, squinting her eyes. "I mean . . . what if this whole thing was a hoax of some kind?"

"Now, now," Longarm said, placing his hands on the girl's shoulders. "I doubt it was any hoax. Me—I'm gonna get to the bottom of this here mystery. I'm damn sure there's a reasonable explanation."

"Don't know what it could be," Wilborn said, rising up on the balls of his boots and hooking his thumbs behind his cartridge belts. "Maybe Miss Sarah's right, Custis. Maybe the whole thing is a hoax."

Longarm slid an even more anxious gaze from the Hell Creek marshal back to him. He squeezed her shoulders reassuringly. "Maybe it is, maybe it ain't. I have a feeling you own a ranch around here, Miss Sarah, and first thing tomorrow we're gonna go out and find it whether anyone knows of your uncle Lester or not."

He glanced at Wilborn, not liking the snide half smile on the man's blond-mustached lips. "Come on. Let's let the girl rest."

He left his gear in room 8 next to the girl's room, then locked the door and pocketed the key with his double-barrel derringer. Sarah watched him worriedly from her own open door.

"You won't go far, will you, Longarm?" she called as he and Wilborn tramped back down the shadowy hall.

Longarm stopped and turned back to her. "I'll be right downstairs if you need anything, Miss Sarah. Just give a yell."

When she'd gone back inside her room and closed

the door, Longarm turned to start down the stairs, the Hell Creek marshal falling into step beside him. Wilborn kept his voice low, his spurs jangling on the steps, as he said with a cockeyed grin, "You and Miss Sarah get sorta . . . well . . . *close* out on the trail, Custis?"

"Close enough so's I care what happens to her," Longarm said. He turned and gave the local badge-toter a pointed look. "Close enough I'm going to get to the bottom of ole Uncle Lester, and close enough I'm going to see that she's safe and sound before I'll even consider leaving your fair little town, Jared."

"If you ain't careful, Custis, I'm gonna start thinkin' you don't trust me!"

Longarm bellied up to the bar. The barman, Ned Charles, stood glowering at him over the glass he was drying with a scrap of dirty towel. Longarm popped the cork on the bottle he'd bought and splashed a shot into one of the two glasses beside it. "If you remember anything about me from our little dance over Nevada way a few years back, you'll remember I don't trust a fucking soul."

He filled his own shot glass and threw back the whiskey. It merely burned his tonsils, didn't shear both of them off like rusty barbed wire, as he'd expected. He refilled Wilborn's and his own glasses then turned to face the man, resting his elbow on the bar edge and holding his glass between the thumb and index finger of that hand. "Tell me, Jared—you know anything about a Lawyer Daggett hereabouts?"

Wilborn was facing the bar, his eyes on the filled shot glass that he was slowly raising to his lips. "Daggett?"

"Why is it I have to say every name twice?" Longarm asked, hearing the impatience growing in his own voice. "Is every Hell Creek citizen hard of hearing?"

Wilborn threw back half his shot and shook his head, flushing with exasperation. "I don't believe anyone's more hard of hearin' that I am, damnit, Custis! No, I don't know of no Lawyer Daggett, just like I don't know of no Uncle Lester, neither. Maybe it's high time you started wondering if there's somethin' a little pulpy in the girl's noggin."

Wilborn turned toward Longarm and lifted his eyes to the stamped tin ceiling. "Pretty as she is, maybe she's a little corky between the ears. You know—crazy as a moonstruck wildcat? Possibly, just possibly, she only *thinks* she's got an uncle Lester. And only *thinks* Uncle Lester done deeded her over his ranch." Wilborn threw back the last of his shot and made a face. "Jesus H. Christ, Ned, that's rotgut stuff!"

He set the glass on the bar, ignoring the glower that the barman had turned on him, and returned his slightly rheumy gaze to Longarm once more. "Don't you think it's all a little fishy?"

"What's a little fishy?"

"Some old rock breaker sendin' his long-lost niece the deed to his ranch way out here in Wyoming? And not just *anywhere* in Wyoming but the backside of *Nowhere*, Wyoming?"

"So she's crazy, that's what I'm supposed to believe?"

"Either that," interjected the barman bravely, "or everyone in Hell Creek is a lyin' son of a bitch!"

Longarm turned to the man. Charles's handsome,

mustached face was flushed with indignation. He shifted his head back a little from Longarm's steely-eyed stare, as though worried he might get slapped.

"Sorry," he said, meekly averting his gaze, dim sunlight from the windows flashing in his round spectacles. "I just don't like bein' called a liar, that's all, Marshal."

Longarm filled and threw back another shot. "Damn, that *is* pretty bad." He slid the bottle toward Wilborn. "Here ya go, Jared. Go blind on me. I'm gonna take a stroll to clear the cobwebs."

"Gonna be rainin' soon, Custis."

Longarm looked out over the batwings. Big, gray thunderheads, heaped like massive airborne boulders, were sliding toward Hell Creek on a freshening breeze. Thunder rumbled distantly. "I ain't afraid of a little rain," the federal lawman said, and pushed through the batwings.

He crossed the porch and hit the street walking, scowling beneath his hat brim.

Chapter 17

Longarm took a long, thoughtful walk around the town, occasionally detouring off Hell Street and walking among the mostly boarded up and abandoned miners' shacks lining the gurgling creek. Here, wolf willows, sage, and wildflowers grew thick, and birds winged out from the cracks in the boarded up windows and doors.

A coffee tin was turned upside down over a chimney pipe, and it clattered against the pipe in the rising wind.

Thunder rumbled, growing gradually louder as the storm made its way up canyon, dimming the afternoon light. The sky began spitting and then, when the rain began hammering, Longarm, who now found himself back on Hell Street, stepped beneath the roof of a porch slanting off the front of what remained of an old harness shop. A cat spooked from behind a barrel abutting the store's front door, and slithered in a yellow-brown blur around the building's far side and into a trash-strewn alley.

Longarm dug into his coat pocket for a cheroot. He bit the twist off the cigar's small end, snapped a match aflame with his thumbnail, and, shielding the flame with his cupped hand, touched it to the large end of the smoke. He blew the acrid but pleasing smoke into the cool wind, staring across the street and into the gap between a small saloon, with a faded sign over its roofless porch, and a mining supply store.

His mind wasn't on the gap littered with old Long Toms and rotting lumber, however. It was on Sarah Hunter's predicament.

If it was indeed her predicament and not his own.

Maybe Wilborn was right. Maybe the girl really was crazier than a tree full of owls. Maybe the deaths of her entire family in that deadly twister had done her in, and she'd only imagined she had an uncle Lester and that Uncle Lester had sent her the deed to the ranch that she had also imagined.

No. That couldn't be right. Longarm himself had seen the deed. True, it had been crudely written in ink, and the paper itself hadn't looked all that official when he thought back on it, but he was sure that what he'd seen was a genuine deed. Of course, he'd felt no need to study on it at the time.

She certainly hadn't drawn the deed up herself, after all.

Had she?

Who knew what a bright young woman who'd been driven crazy by grief was capable of doing? He'd known several crazy people over his career, and he'd known a few who'd done some pretty bizarre, spectacular things. He'd known several who were as much the butt of their own elaborate ruses as anyone else.

Maybe that was the case with Sarah.

The wind picked up, blowing rain under the porch roof at Longarm. He gave his back to it and walked over to stand at the building's far front corner around which the cat had fled. Sticking the cheroot in his mouth, he took a deep drag and stared into the break before him.

He frowned as he let the cigar smoke trickle out of his mouth and nostrils, then stepped down off the end of the porch and walked over to where an old wooden sign and a peeled log pine pole lay on the ground beside the building on the break's far side. Dropping to a knee, Longarm lifted the sign out of the sage and gravel and turned it over until the badly faded words HOMER H. P. DAGGETT, ATTORNEY AT LAW glared up at him from the sign flecked with weathered green paint. The words were like little daggers drilling into his skull through his eyes.

On the sign's upper left corner was a painted hand with an extended index finger pointing up.

Longarm turned to stare down the gap. An outside stairs halfway down the gap rose to a nondescript door in the second story of the harness shop. Longarm glanced at the sign again. Then at the pole. Looking over his right shoulder, he saw the relatively fresh gouges in a post supporting the harness shop's porch roof, marking where the sign had been torn down.

Longarm would have bet silver cartwheels to stale

donuts that the hand on the sign had been pointing up toward the door at the top of the stairs.

He looked around, squinting against the rain slashing at him though he was relatively protected by the harness shop. Seeing no one on Hell Street, he clamped his hat down tighter on his head, jogged down the alley, and climbed the stairs. He twisted the rusty metal doorknob and was a little surprised to feel it turn easily and the door sag inward.

The hinges squawked. As he pushed the door farther open, warm, stale air pushed against him, bearing the faint scent of leather, wood varnish, and pipe smoke.

"Hello?" Longarm called as he stepped into an office outfitted with a worn, red-and-gray Oriental rug, a rolltop desk, and several file cabinets and bookcases. "Anyone here?"

He doubted anyone was here. Least of all Lawyer Daggett.

He stood on the rug, facing into the office, and pushed the door closed behind him. When it latched with a click, he reached to his left and sprung the paper shade hanging down over the window, allowing some gray light to push the shadows back farther into the room. He moved around, quickly inspecting the main office and two back rooms—a bedroom and small kitchen—before giving his attention to the rolltop desk.

There was a green-shaded Tiffany lamp on the desk, beside a pipe rack, a small leather sack of pipe tobacco, and a wood carving of a shaggy dog. Longarm peered into the desk's stuffed pigeonholes. He was only vaguely aware of what he was looking for until he found it a few minutes later—the name "LESTER DEBO" written in blue-black ink on the tab of a file folder in one of the file cabinets.

Longarm's heart quickened as he pulled out the folder and opened it. Frustration nipped him when he saw the folder was empty. He returned the folder to the drawer, closed the drawer, and, chewing his mustache, turned to the window that was beaded with rain.

For the past several minutes, since the wind had kicked up, he'd been hearing a banging sound coming from somewhere outside. Now he went over to the window and turned to stare right along the alley, in the direction of the wooden din.

From this angle, and through the rain, he could barely make out the outline of a privy flanking the building housing the harness shop and Lawyer Daggett's office. The wind was waving the privy door back and forth, slamming it wildly against its frame.

Longarm went out, snugged his hat down tight against the wind, and strode out to the privy that abutted a stack of split stovewood. He grabbed the door and held it before him. In the middle of the door was a ragged, pumpkin-sized hole. Longarm knew a buckshot hole when he saw one.

He opened the door and peered into the privy, squinting against the dimness. Finally, he could clearly see what looked like a massive stain of blood and gore on the wall above and behind the latrine's single hole.

He released the door, stepped into the outhouse, and

leaned forward over the hole. The smell of rotten flesh made his eyes water. He could see bits of torn cloth clinging to the blood and gore, some of which had dried in drips down the privy's vertical boards. Much of the buckshot had drilled through the man who'd been sitting here and had continued on through the back wall.

Judging by how dry the stain was, Lawyer Daggett had been blasted to Kingdom Come at least a couple of weeks ago. Maybe more. Still, the sweet stench of decay was overwhelming. It was too strong for the amount of blood and viscera pasted against the wall.

Longarm stepped even farther forward and dropped his gaze down the hole. He canted his head left and right, letting some light in around him, until the unmistakable figure of a human body showed itself among the muck of the privy hole. Lawyer Daggett reposed nearly vertically, head down, bent legs canted against the sides of the pit. Longarm could clearly see a gold belt buckle and the tip of a brown shoe. There was a dull glint of pale, naked flesh.

Shot in his own privy and shoved down the hole.

Longarm turned and walked back outside. He closed the door then heaved it snug in its frame and looked around. His heart was beating regularly, but each beat was a hammering blow against his ribs.

He hated murder. But he especially hated cold-blooded murder. And there was no more cold-blooded way to kill a man than to blast him while he's sitting in his own privy. Taking not only his life but his dignity.

Who had committed such a cowardly crime?

Longarm started back up the alley along the side of the harness shop. The rain slanted against him though it was somewhat broken by the shop itself rising on his left. He was halfway to Hell Street when someone stepped out from behind the front of the building on his right, stopped there at the corner, half in front of the building and half in the alley, and stared at him.

Long, damp, red-silver hair blew around the craggy face in the wind. Kay Adams held a shawl about her shoulders as she regarded him obliquely for about two seconds then quickly retreated back behind the front of the building on Longarm's right again.

"Hey!" Longarm called above the wind.

He ran forward and turned the corner just as the woman ran into her café, long hair and the tail of her shawl streaming out behind her.

"Hold on, Mrs. Adams!"

Longarm strode past the front of a closed drugstore. The café was just beyond it. When Longarm gained the mud puddle fronting the eatery's door, he reached for the doorknob but did not turn it. A CLOSED TILL SUPPERTIME sign jostled from a rusty nail in the door.

He glanced toward the window left of the door at the same time a pale, gnarled hand pulled a shade down over it.

"All right," Longarm said, stepping back out of the muddy water filling the depression in front of the door. "All right. We'll talk later, Mrs. Adams." Wincing against the slashing rain that was quickly soaking him—why hadn't he worn his slicker?—he lifted the

collar of his frock coat to his jaws and looked around
at the mostly abandoned Hell Street with its buildings
of every shape and proportion. Rain splashed the growing puddles in the street's copper-colored mud.

He doubted that Kay Adams had shotgunned Lawyer
Daggett and thrown him down his privy. Most likely a
man did that. Mrs. Adams knew who had done the dirty
deed, however. Probably every remaining soul in town
did. He felt like rounding them all up, corralling them
in the saloon, and asking them the burning question
collectively. Several burning questions, in fact.

Who had murdered Daggett?

Why had they murdered him?

Why were they pretending not to know anything
about Uncle Lester and his ranch?

Something told Longarm that direct approach would
do him little good. Something told him he might have
a hell of a fight on his hands and that Sarah might get
caught in the cross fire. He wasn't overly concerned
about her now. Doubtless, anyone gunning for her would
likely try to take Longarm out of the equation first.

He'd wait till he had her safely ensconced at her uncle's ranch—if they could find the place, that was. Then
he'd return to Hell Creek and start questioning its citizens, starting with its town marshal, Jared Wilborn. For
now, he'd keep quiet about Daggett. Let the remaining
Hell Creek populace do the wondering and squirming
for a change.

Wondering about what Longarm's own next move
would be. Mrs. Adams would no doubt spread word that

he'd found Daggett's shotgunned carcass, and that would likely set them squirming in earnest.

Soaked, feeling his nerves twitching around just beneath his skin, Longarm slogged back to the saloon. He needed to get dry and a little drunk.

Chapter 18

In the Hell Creek Saloon's main drinking hall, since there were no respectable ladies around for him to offend with his indiscreet behavior—Sarah was upstairs napping after her bath—Longarm stripped down to his balbriggans and hung his clothes over a couple of chair backs to dry. There was no fire in the woodstove as, despite the storm, it wasn't cold enough for that, so it would likely take a while for the duds to dry.

Longarm didn't care. He wasn't going anywhere until the next day.

Clad in only his hat, boots, and long underwear, a cigar smoldering between his teeth, he sat at a table in the middle of the room, positioned so that he could see the back stairs as well as the front door. He had his Colt .44 snugged down in its open-toed holster and strapped around his waist. His fully loaded Winchester '73 resided across the table near his right hand.

Kicked back in his chair, he smoked and nursed a bottle of the particularly foul brand of label-less rotgut that Ned Charles served in his crude establishment. The lack of quality liquor was understandable, for Charles had no competitors here in Hell Creek, though Longarm reflected, while he smoked and drank and watched the waxing and waning of the mountain monsoon out the saloon's front windows, that if he himself resided here he'd brew his own forty-rod in the handiest stock trough.

Whatever he could come up with would have to be at least as good as what Ned Charles charged two dollars a bottle for. He'd have given his right ball to see ole Tom Moore staring out at him from a Maryland rye label.

All afternoon, he was the only customer. Occasionally, he curled his lip at that. He hadn't seen anyone on the street before the saloon, but he had a feeling that somehow Kay Adams had managed to spread the word about the federal badge-toter's visit to Lawyer Daggett's privy. Despite the storm, the town was eerily quiet. It was as though God were holding his breath, waiting for something to happen.

Even Ned Charles, who couldn't possibly have gotten the word from Mrs. Adams without Longarm knowing, seemed edgy as he spent the afternoon sweeping his clean floor or playing himself at cribbage, whistling and softly tapping one brown shoe on the floor beneath his table near the bar. Occasionally the man would roll his eyes to the side and turn his head a little, glancing at Longarm over his left shoulder before returning his attention to his cribbage board and his flat beer.

Longarm had just poured himself another drink when he heard the light tread of female feet on the stairs. Turning, he saw Sarah coming down the steps in her traveling outfit, looking scrubbed and fresh, her brushed hair fairly glowing as it curved down her shoulders. She turned her face to him and chuckled, covering her mouth with her hand.

"Longarm, what on earth . . . ?"

"Got a little wet when I was trampin' around the town earlier, Miss Sarah. Please forgive me."

She chuckled again with embarrassment, and as she reached the bottom of the stairs, she stared straight ahead, flushing. She'd seen him a whole lot more naked than this, of course. And they'd been a hell of a lot closer together than they were now. Her discomfiture was because Ned Charles didn't know that, and in a town that she hoped would become her home soon, she had to keep up appearances. It didn't take much for a girl to acquire a reputation. Rooming in a saloon alone would do it—if the town had any other rooms available. Since Hell Creek didn't, she likely wouldn't have to wear any scarlet letters on her breast.

"Just keep your eyes down, Miss Sarah," Longarm said for the barman's benefit, as he gathered his nearly dry duds off the chairs. "Wouldn't want you to get the vapors or nothin' and pass out."

When he was once again decent, Sarah said she was hungry. Longarm looked out over the batwings, setting his rifle on his shoulder. The rain had passed and the sun was peeking out from behind the remaining clouds,

flashing brilliantly in the puddles the storm had left
behind.

"Let's mosey on over to Mrs. Adams's place," Longarm said, hooking his arm for the girl. "I saw by her
sign she's open for supper."

He could do with a meal himself, and he was going
to enjoy watching the café owner squirm. He wasn't sure
that Mrs. Adams had seen him come out of the privy,
but she had to know from seeing him walking away
from it that he'd likely inspected the last resting place
of Lawyer Daggett.

As he and Sarah made their way down the muddy
street toward the café, meandering around puddles, she
said, "Did you find out anything about Uncle Lester,
Longarm?"

"Nah, I'm sorry, girl. We'll just have to follow the
information on your deed and find the place ourselves.
I'm sure there's a reasonable explanation for all this."

He'd considered informing her that her life might very
well be in danger, but he couldn't bring himself to do it.
He didn't know how she'd react to such information, and
he didn't want to chance her going hysterical on him and
making their visit to the Hell Creek country all the more
difficult. He also didn't want Jared Wilborn or anyone
else in town to know exactly how much he knew about
the dastardly doings here.

Better to keep them nervous and wondering. Nervous, curious folks usually had the disadvantage in a
dangerous situation.

As for Sarah, he'd stay as close to her as possible until
the trouble here in Hell Creek had played itself out. That

shouldn't be hard. Maintaining his professionalism, however, might be another matter altogether.

The shade over the café window had been lifted, and the sign on the door had been turned to OPEN. Longarm led Sarah inside. Kay Adams stood at the stove, one fist on a skinny hip, briskly scraping potatoes and onions around in a large cast-iron skillet. As Longarm stolled into the café and Sarah closed the door behind him, Mrs. Adams turned toward him and frowned, working her thin lips thoughtfully.

"Somethin' sure smells good," Longarm said, removing his hat and casting the woman a friendly smile.

His manner seemed to befuddle her. She turned back to her work, muttering to herself beneath the sizzling of the potatoes and the onions. Longarm saw that the older gent and the younger gent he'd seen in the café earlier—George and Billy—had taken the same table they'd had before at the back of the room.

The two half-breed liverymen sat at the first table nearest the door. That left two free tables. Longarm didn't like the idea of giving his back to anyone in Hell Creek, but he had no choice.

He sat in a chair at the table nearest the half-breeds, his back to them, while Sarah sat in the chair opposite, her back to George and Billy. Longarm made a show of leaning his Winchester against the table near his chair. Both parties were scowling at him and Sarah from beneath their brows, not looking one bit happy. Likely, Mrs. Adams had informed them about Longarm's visit to Lawyer Daggett's privy.

He smiled and nodded to both men then sagged back
in his chair, feigning peace of mind but not letting his
right hand stray too far from his .44. None of the four
in the café appeared to be wearing a sidearm, but that
didn't mean they didn't have one or two, maybe a knife,
hidden somewhere on their scruffy persons.

He kept his eyes and ears skinned as Mrs. Adams
served the half-breeds plates of elk steak and potatoes,
then refilled the coffee cups of George and Billy. She
seemed in no hurry to serve Longarm and Sarah. When
she'd returned the coffeepot to the range, Longarm called
to her jovially, "What's our choices tonight, Mrs Adams?"

"Elk steak and potatoes." She grouched, forking a
couple of steaks from a pan on the stove's warming rack
onto two tin plates then shoveling greasy potatoes and
onions on and around them.

"Damn, if that don't look like some o' the best vittles
I've ever seen!" Longarm intoned, rubbing his hands
together eagerly as the old woman shuffled over and
slammed the plates down before him and Sarah.

"Ain't no different than what you had a few hours
ago," the woman grumbled as she turned away, wiping
her hands on her apron.

"Coffee, please," Sarah said.

"It's comin'!"

Sarah leaned toward Longarm. "What's wrong with
her? She was very pleasant earlier."

"Off her feed, I reckon," Longarm said, cutting into
the thick, charred chunk of elk.

He was glad when the two half-breeds, Crow and his
stocky lackey, whom he'd heard Mrs. Adams call Vin-

cent, finished their meals and left the café. George and Billy left next, both eyeing Longarm and Sarah darkly as they dropped some coins onto their table then stomped to the front door.

Longarm and Sarah finished their own meals a few minutes behind George and Billy. While Mrs. Adams made a show of being preoccupied with washing dishes in a deep vat of hot water and sudsy lye soap, Longarm and Sarah paid for their supper. "Thanks, Mrs. Adams," Longarm called as he and Sarah made for the door. "See ya bright and early for breakfast."

"Oh, you will, will ya?" he could just barely hear her mutter above the splashing of her dishwater.

She didn't look up. Longarm took special note of her tone and the possible warning in her words. That's why, as he escorted Sarah back toward the saloon and the sun drifted down behind the tall western ridges, he said, "Miss Sarah, please don't take this as a play for more of what we had before . . . uh, back in the cave. But I do believe I'm going to share your room tonight."

She glanced up at him, arching a brow, a faintly lusty smile quirking her pink lips. "I know it's naughty of me, Longarm, but I can't help thinking of that night. And I would like nothing more than to repeat it. But do you think that wise here in Hell Creek? I wouldn't want anyone to think me . . . uh, well . . . *wanton*."

"Like I said, I'm not making a play to compromise your reputation. I just have a sense it might be wise if I remained close to you."

Her frown deepened, and her eyes became con-cerned. "You think I'm in danger here, don't you?"

Longarm stopped and placed his hands on her shoulders. "How strong are you, Miss Sarah?"

She studied him for a moment, fear glinting in her eyes. Then she hardened her jaws, swallowed, and met his graze directly as she said, "As tough as I need to be, Longarm."

"All right, then. Yes, I think you might be in danger. I think the town for whatever reason is out to get Uncle Lester's ranch. I have no idea why. But there it is."

"And you think they might . . . ?" She wrinkled her brows, incredulous, and shook her head. "You think they might actually try to harm me. *Kill* me?"

"It's a possibility," he said recultantly. No need to tell her yet about Lawyer Daggett. For now, she knew enough.

Chapter 19

Sarah went up to her room as soon as she and Longarm returned to the Hell Creek Saloon.

Longarm stayed up for a couple of hours, playing a game of poker with Wilborn, Ned Charles, Crow, and both George and Billy, who, Longarm learned, were father and son. George was the father. He and Billy lived in their old shack out by the creek. George was a sullen drunk and grumbler, not to mention poor poker player, and Billy, only slightly better at the game, had a wandering left eye.

Crow's lackey, Vincent, sat at a table by the window, alone. All evening, the stocky barn swamper leaned low over his table, studying a yellowed newspaper spread out before him, squinting and moving his lips, as though reading the old paper were a devil of a job that he was bound and determined to tackle.

No one mentioned Longarm's visit to Lawyer

Daggett's privy, but the subject hovered over the saloon as the storm had earlier.

Around ten-thirty, Longarm yawned and stretched and said he was going to tumble on into the old mattress sack; then he went upstairs, keeping his head sort of turned to one side so he could detect any sudden movement behind him. He had a strong feeling that Hell Creek's remaining citizens would love nothing better than to do to him what they, or at least one of them, had done to Lawyer Daggett.

Longarm made sure no one was lurking in the second-floor hall before he poked his key in the lock of Sarah's door. When he heard the locking bolt click, he pushed the door open quickly and stepped into the room. He closed the door quietly, so as not to wake the girl, but noticed that a lamp burned on the small room's lone dresser. It cast a dull, pink light, though shadows prevailed.

"Holy, shi—!" he said with a start, when he'd turned to the bed and saw that Sarah was not asleep, as he'd expected.

Rather, she lay belly down on the bed's top quilt, her head toward him, feet nearest the far wall. She'd put her hair up and taken every stitch of her clothes off. Naked as a newborn babe but considerably more filled out, she smiled up at him over the brass bed frame that rose only a few feet away from him.

Longarm drew a slow breath and felt his heart thud as he ran his eyes down from the girl's smiling, green-eyed face to her pale breasts sloping toward the mattress beneath her, pink nipples brushing the quilt. He slid his gaze from her beautiful tits—a double handful, each—

to her slender back and flaring hips and the beguiling swell of her creamy ass.

She had her legs bent over her back, ankles crossed. She flexed her little, pink toes and dug her fingertips catlike into the quilt as she said, "I was too afraid to sleep, so I decided to wait for you." Her cheeks dimpled as she dropped her chin and lifted her eyes with false demureness. "It's hot."

"Miss Sarah, it ain't hot, and you do not look afraid at all."

"Oh, but I am. Or . . ." She gave a coy smile. "I was but then I started to think about you, and I felt as safe as a newborn lamb in a manger. And then a bad feeling came over me . . . when I remembered . . . *lying* with you . . . in the *cave*."

She dropped her eyes to his crotch. Likely, she saw the growing bulge.

"Oh, God, Longarm, I've become so depraved. I don't mean to. Honest! It's just that I . . . I never had a man before you"—she dug her fingers into the quilt again as though trying to claw holes in it—"and I didn't realize how sick with the need I was!"

Longarm turned back to the door and turned the key in the lock, and left it there. He leaned his rifle against the dresser, in easy reach from the bed, then tossed his hat onto a hide-bottom chair. He stared down at her as he unbuckled his gun belt then buckled it again and looped it over a front bedpost. Meanwhile, the girl rolled onto her side, enticing wisps of blond hair dangling across her cheeks that were flushed with desire. Lying there, with the lamplight caressing her beautiful body, she was the very picture of womanly ripeness and femininity.

Longarm sat on the edge of the bed, lowered his head to her bottom, and pressed his lips to her hip. Doing so, feeling his cock harden, he told himself he had to keep his ears peeled for movement on the stairs and in the hall. This was surely crazy, but he couldn't help himself. Maybe it would be wisest to go ahead and give the girl the fucking she so desired so he could return his attention to keeping her . . . and him . . . alive.

He ran a hand down the length of her smooth left thigh then rose and kicked out of his boots and shucked off his coat, shirt, vest, and whipcord trousers. His cock was protruding from the fly of his balbriggans. Before he could peel the long underwear down his brawny frame, Sarah reached out from the bed and squeezed his jutting shaft. She squirmed and groaned, grinding her knees together as she squeezed him harder.

Her nipples were pebbled and distended.

"Oh, God, I want that big thing inside me, Longarm!" she said and mewled.

Longarm wrestled his way out of the balbriggans then crouched over the girl, rolled her onto her back, and spread her legs. He mashed his face against her silky snatch and nuzzled her, probing her cunt with his tongue, while she writhed on the bed, clamping both her hands over her mouth lest anyone else in the building should hear her and think she was getting mauled by a rampaging grizzly.

Or, worse—fucking a man she was not married to!

When he had her on the edge of fulfillment, he withdrew his tongue and pressed it to her belly button. He slid it up across her belly to her breasts. He licked and sucked her nipples until they were nearly as large and hard as sewing thimbles.

Now she was groaning and rocking and fairly spasming, spreading her legs as far as she could, grinding her heels into his back and begging him with her eyes to finish her.

He shoved his raging hard-on into her wet pussy, and, working as quietly and slowly as he could, carried them both off across the ocean of bliss toward sexual oblivion. When he'd gone at it for ten minutes or so, and he could tell by the way her cunt was clutching at him while the rest of her body fairly convulsed, sweat dribbling down her cheeks, that she was near the end, he heard the creak of a loose floorboard in the hall.

He looked up while he continued to plunder the girl.

A shadow moved under the door.

Sarah lifted her head, gritted her teeth, and squeezed her eyes closed as she said, "*Ahhhh, gawwwwwww—!*"

The door burst open and slammed against the wall.

Longarm already had his Colt in his hand and was squeezing the double-action trigger, drawing the hammer back to full cock, when he saw the hatted, blond-mustached figure bolt into the room, extending a double-barrel shotgun straight out from his right hip. Longarm's Colt leaped and roared. The man in the doorway screamed and flew straight back as the shotgun jerked up and rocked the entire building with its blast, both barrels stabbing flames at the ceiling.

Plaster rained as the figure fell to the hall floor with

a thud that was nearly inaudible beneath the still-echoing blast of the shotgun.

Again, the bushwhacker screamed, groaned.

Sarah stared up at Longarm, her mouth wide but issuing no sound whatever. Expressions running from unadulterated ecstasy to bald horror passed across her bright eyes. She wasn't facing the door so she hadn't seen what Longarm had been shooting at; she'd only heard the cacophony that had seemingly exploded from their simultaneous climax.

Longarm's cock spurted once more into the girl. Then he pulled it out of her, climbed off the bed, and dashed into the hall. On the floor, Jared Wilborn writhed and gritted his teeth as blood pumped from the hole in his chest.

He glared up at the big naked man standing over him. "You . . . kilt me, Custis . . . ya son of a bitch!"

He'd barely got that last out before the light left his eyes and his body fell still as stone, his hands dropping to the floor.

"*Sonnnnn!*" came a shrill, tooth-gnashing screech from the end of the hall toward the stairs.

Longarm whipped around to see Kay Adams standing at the top of the stairs, her ugly face a mask of rage and horror, eyes nearly popping out of her death-pale face. She raised both fists, and the wan lamplight from the drinking hall glinted on the pocket pistols in her gnarled hands.

"Don't do it!" Longarm shouted.

Too late. She'd gotten both hoglegs leveled, and he

had no choice but to drill her, crouching and firing, his Colt leaping twice in his own fist.

She screamed and fired one of the pistols into the floor as she stumbled back against the wall. She bounced off the wall, gave another scream, fired her second pistol into the post at the top of the stairs, then fell sideways to her right and out of Longarm's sight.

But he could hear the crunching thuds as the café owner tumbled down the stairs.

Longarm clicked back the Colt's hammer, crouched and ready, whipping his head to peer down toward the opposite end of the hall, wary of another would-be shooter. He was only vaguely conscious that he was naked and that his dick was still wet from his and Sarah's coupling. He had more important things to worry about.

Silence fell over the building. Then a man's voice, pitched low with awe, sounded on the saloon's ground floor. There was the faint ching of a spur.

Again, Longarm looked behind him, making sure no one was sneaking up from the other end of the hall, then strode quickly to the stairs and looked down. He extended the Colt out in front of him, angled down toward where Kay Adams lay sprawled on her back at the bottom, a blood pool growing beneath her, two holes gushing the red fluid from her chest.

Her eyes were open and bizarrely staring, thin lips stretched back from her teeth in a death snarl.

Longarm kept the Colt aimed down the stairs even when he saw that all the men gathered around her—Ned Charles, Crow, Vincent, George, and Billy—were not holding weapons in their hands. The somber group stood staring down at Mrs. Adams then, one at a time, lifted their heads to peer up at Longarm.

They were all dull-eyed with exasperation. Their eyes flicked up and down Longarm's big frame, and then he remembered once more that he was naked.

Still, he had more important things to worry about.

He narrowed an angry eye as he stared down his Colt's barrel. "What's the matter—the game too rich for the rest of you?"

They all just stared at him for a time.

Then Ned Charles shook his head and rubbed his hands nervously across his apron. "We was never in on their game, Marshal. Kay and her boy—they were the only ones."

"Wilborn was her son?"

Charles nodded while the others stared dully up at Longarm. "She came here to run the café when her brothel burned down in Crow Feather. She and Jared came with the boom, didn't have money to get out with the bust. Then we all found out a spur-line railroad was gonna be put through just north of here, connecting Crow Feather with Willow Creek higher up in the mountains. Big boom up there. Gold. Silver. Copper. The whole shebang."

Longarm depressed the Colt's hammer and lowered the weapon. "So?"

"They're gonna run the line through Lester Debo's place. We all figured the rail line would buy him out for way more than the land was really worth, like they usually do. So, when Lester died after a horse kicked him last fall, Kay and Jared got the idea of takin' over his ranch. They'd heard he didn't have no family out this way and damn few anywhere else. Jared was gonna finagle some figures, say Lester owed back taxes on it, and he and his ma was gonna pay the taxes for the quit-claim. Then they'd sell it to the railroad."

Charles smiled grimly. "Though I doubted they really woulda paid those taxes, don't ya know. Since Jared was the only law out here, he and his ma could get away with pretty much whatever they pleased. Only, they didn't know Lester had willed the ranch to his niece until they heard Lawyer Daggett talkin' about it right here in my saloon, about a month ago."

Longarm gave a wry chuff. "So they killed Daggett and destroyed his file on Uncle Lester. Warned you and the rest of Hell Creek's citizens that if his niece actually made it to Hell Creek alive, to keep quiet about her uncle. Pretend you'd never heard of him."

"Or they'd kill us," said Billy's pa, George. "They'd shotgun us and throw us down our own privies, just like Wilborn did to Lawyer Daggett when Daggett balked at their plan. I'm sure they figured if they had to, they'd kill the girl themselves. They just hadn't been countin' on her bein' escorted here by a federal marshal."

The barman said, "That killer they sent out after her was Wilborn's cousin, Tom Wilborn. Son of Kay's twin sister. You mighta run into him." He gave another wry smile with half of his mouth.

"Well, I'll be damned," Longarm said, growing a little more self-conscious about his state of undress, "I didn't know ole Jared was so tight with his kin. Never knew that about him." Feeling his ears warm a little, he covered his dangling cock with his hand and turned away then stopped and turned back. "So . . . that spur line still gonna be put through Lester Debo's ranch?"

"Far as we know," Charles said.

"Well, I'll be damned," Longarm said, starting down the hall.

He stopped when he saw Sarah standing with her back against the hall's right wall, holding a blanket over her breasts and looking stricken. Light emanated from her door a few yards away, but she was mostly in shadow.

Longarm put his hand on her bare shoulder. "You hear that, girl?"

"I heard everything." She nodded dully, frowning, as though still trying to wrap her mind around all that had happened this evening, starting with the raucous interruption of her and Longarm's torrid lovemaking.

She turned to look at Jared Wilborn lying crumpled in front of her open door, blood oozing out around him. "My God, Custis—I thought it was all just stories made up by crazy writers."

"What was?"

"The West. It really is quite wild, isn't it?"

"In some places it shore is. When you get that money for Uncle Lester's ranch, you can go back to Minnesota, where it's a little more quiet."

She looked up at him, glassy-eyed. "You know, I might like that."

Longarm chuckled, wrapped his arm around her waist, and led her back to her room. "Come on, dear

Sarah. I think I know how to get your mind off all this wildness."

"Will you stay with me, Custis?" she said as he closed the door behind them. "Until I get the money and can go home and buy another farm? I would very much love to spend more time with you. Quieter times."

She lifted her mouth corners and regarded him devilishly from beneath her brows.

"Well, I don't know . . ."

"I'll make it worth your while." She dropped the blanket.

"Ah hell," Longarm said, feasting his eyes on her and getting randy all over again. "I reckon I can tell Billy Vail that due to the summer storms—not to mention *lead* storms!—it took me an extra long time to get that stolen mail train money back to Utah."

He placed his hands on her breasts and nuzzled her neck.

"Oh, Custis!"

Watch for

LONGARM AND LUCKY LUCY

the 403rd novel in the exciting LONGARM
series from Jove

Coming in June!